MEET THE GIRL TALK CHARACTERS

Sabrina Wells is petite, with curly auburn hair, sparkling hazel eyes, and a bubbly personality. Sabrina loves magazines, shopping, sleepovers, and most of all, she loves talking to her best friends.

Katie Campbell is a straight-A student and super athlete. With her blond hair, blue eyes, and matching clothes, she's everyone's idea of Little Miss Perfect. But Katie has a few surprises for everyone, including herself!

Randy Zak has just moved to Acorn Falls from New York City, and is she ever cool! With her radical spiked haircut and her hip New York clothes, Randy teaches everyone just how much fun it is to be different.

Allison Cloud is a Native American Indian. Allison's supersmart and really beautiful. But she has one major problem: She's thirteen years old, five foot seven, and still growing!

Thanks to Ali R. for a great idea.

ALLISON'S BABY-SITTING
ADVENTURE

By L. E. Blair

GIRL TALK® series created by Western Publishing Company, Inc.

Western Publishing Company, Inc., Racine, Wisconsin 53404

Text by B. B. Calhoun

Chapter One

"Let's see," said Sabrina, peering inside her locker. "Maybe if I take out just a few more things..."

It was Wednesday morning, just before homeroom, and Sabrina Wells, one of my best friends, was staring into her locker at Bradley Junior High, looking exasperated. My name's Allison Cloud and Sabrina and I, along with our other best friends, Randy Zak and Katie Campbell, are all in the seventh grade at Bradley.

"What are you doing, Sabs?" I asked, looking at the pile of books and papers on the floor around her.

She held up a long black case with a metal handle.

"Band practice day, Allison," she said, her auburn curls bouncing. "I'm trying to get my clarinet in my locker so I don't have to lug it around to all my classes."

1

I shook my head. It's kind of amazing that Sabs and Katie can share the locker at all, considering that Katie is the organized, superneat type and Sabs always has tons of extra stuff in her locker.

"There!" said Sabrina triumphantly, shoving the black case into the locker at last. She looked up at us and smiled, her hazel eyes twinkling.

"Great, Sabs," said Randy. She grinned and ran her hand through her spiky black hair. "Now I guess you just have to figure out what to do with all the rest of that stuff."

Sabrina looked at the piles of clothes, books, and papers on the floor around her and wrinkled her forehead.

"Oh," she said. "I kind of forgot about all of that."

At that moment I saw Katie walking down the hall toward us. She was wearing an off-white parka over a red knit minidress. She also had on white tights, plus dark blue flats and a red ribbon tied around her straight blond ponytail.

"Oh, boy," Katie said with a sigh. She put down her black-and-white-striped book bag and looked at the stuff on the floor in front of the locker. "Is it band practice day again so soon?"

Sabrina looked up at her sheepishly.

"I really thought I could fit it all in this time, Katie," she said.

Katie smiled.

"Okay, Sabs," she said. She pulled off her jacket and straightened her ponytail. "I'll tell you what. Give me your clarinet. I've got some extra space in my part of the locker. Then you can put all this stuff back in your section."

"Wow, thanks," said Sabrina, grinning. She pulled out the clarinet case, causing a ruler and a rubber boot to come flying out with it, and handed it to Katie. "Now, if I can just get the rest of this stuff back in here."

"Here, Sabs. Let me help you," said Randy.

"Something tells me we'd *all* better pitch in if we want to make it to homeroom on time," I said as I bent down to pick up some of the things on the floor.

I have to admit, it was kind of hard for me to just shove all the stuff back in Sabrina's locker like that. I'm more like Katie when it comes to things like my locker — I like everything to be really organized. But I knew we had no choice if we didn't want to be late.

As we stuffed the last of Sabrina's things into

3

the locker, Randy turned to look at me.

"Wow, Allie, cool necklace," she said, looking at the little silver dove, peace sign, and planet Earth that were hanging from a leather cord around my neck.

"Thanks," I said, reaching up to touch the three charms. "Actually, it's Mary's, but she let me borrow it today."

Mary Birdsong is the college student who lives with my family and helps take care of my little brother and sister. She's a Native American Chippewa Indian, like everyone in my family. Mary's really nice, and she has some of the most amazing jewelry I've ever seen.

"That was really cool of her to lend it to you," said Randy.

"Well, she's got this really big psychology exam coming up in a couple of weeks, and I've been helping her study," I said. "She said she was glad to return the favor."

I glanced at my watch. "Come on, you guys," I said. "It's getting late. We'd better get to home-room."

"Okay," said Katie as she helped Sabs push their locker door shut. "There, that ought to do it."

We hurried down the hall to homeroom and slipped into our seats just before the bell rang.

Ms. Staats, who is both our homeroom teacher and our English teacher, was just starting to call attendance. After she finished, the chimes sounded over the loudspeaker, which meant that Mr. Hansen, our principal, was about to make the morning announcements.

As soon as the chimes sounded, Stacy Hansen, who happens to be Mr. Hansen's daughter, and who was sitting in the front row as usual, began shushing everyone around her and telling them to be quiet. You'd think Stacy could leave that job to Ms. Staats, who is, after all, the teacher. Just because her father's the principal, Stacy thinks she can act like she owns the whole school. She and her group of friends, Eva Malone, B. Z. Latimer, and Laurel Spencer, are always acting like they're better than everyone else. Randy, Katie, Sabrina, and I don't get along with them very well.

Everybody quieted down, and the loudspeaker crackled as Mr. Hansen began to speak.

"Good morning, Bradley students," he said.

"Good morning, Bradley students," Sam Wells parroted behind me. Sam is Sabrina's twin brother, and he's a little bit of a class clown.

A couple of kids snickered, and Ms. Staats gave Sam a quick warning look.

The first few announcements weren't really interesting — practice for the boys' softball team had been rescheduled, and some eighth-grade teacher was absent, so a substitute would be taking over her classes. There was also a reminder about band practice that afternoon, which made me think of Sabs's clarinet and smile.

Then Mr. Hansen said, "All right, students. I have one final announcement to make today. It concerns a charity organization called the Magic Star Foundation, which helps grant the wishes of very sick children."

I recognized the name. I had read an article in the newspaper about the Magic Star Foundation the week before.

Mr. Hansen went on.

"Our own local chapter of the Magic Star Foundation has announced its annual Give-a-Thon," he said. "And this year I've agreed to get Bradley involved in the fund-raising effort.

"Magic Star has decided to sponsor a competition here at Bradley," explained Mr. Hansen. "The idea is to see which group of students can raise the most money for the Give-a-Thon. I hope you'll all think about participating, because it's a very good cause. In addition, many people here in Acorn Falls have donated prizes to be awarded to the winning teams. I've passed out some information sheets and registration blanks to your homeroom teachers, so if you're interested in forming a team and participating, please speak to them. That's all for today."

The chimes sounded again, and the loudspeaker went off.

"All right, everyone," said Ms. Staats, picking up a stack of papers on her desk. "I have all the information about the Give-a-Thon right here. Now, a team can be made up of anywhere from two to eight people, and you'll need to register all the members here with me on this form. How you raise the money is up to you, of course, but the deadline for the Give-a-Thon is in three weeks, so make sure you register your teams as soon as possible. I should also tell you that —"

Suddenly Stacy raised her hand.

"Oh, Ms. Staats," she called in the sugary voice she uses with teachers and other grown-ups she wants to impress.

"Yes, Stacy?" said Ms. Staats, looking up from her papers.

"Ms. Staats, I'd like to be the first in our class to volunteer for this worthy cause."

I glanced at Randy, who rolled her eyes. I knew she was thinking the same thing I was thinking — Stacy always has to be the first to do anything in our class. She thinks it makes her special or something.

"Well, that's fine, Stacy," said Ms. Staats. "But you can't register on your own, you know. You'll need to form a team."

"Oh, that's no problem," said Stacy brightly. "Eva Malone, B. Z. Latimer, and Laurel Spencer are all going to be on my team, too."

I couldn't help noticing that Eva, B.Z., and Laurel looked pretty surprised when Stacy said this. After all, there hadn't been any time for them to think about whether they *wanted* to volunteer or not.

"Okay, girls, that's fine," said Ms. Staats, writing in their names on the form in front of her.

I glanced at Randy, Sabs, and Katie. I definitely thought Magic Star sounded like a pretty cool organization, and I wondered if they would be willing to volunteer for this thing. I caught Randy's eye again, and she gave me the thumbs-up sign, nudging Sabrina with her other arm. As Sabs and Katie turned to look at me, I raised my eyebrows, and they both nodded immediately. It still amazed me that my friends and I could have an entire conversation without saying one word.

Just as I raised my hand, Ms. Staats began to talk again.

"Now, let me tell you about the nice prizes for the winning teams," she said, looking down at the papers in front of her. "First prize," she read, "is a rollerblading party at Rob's Rollers. Second prize is a certificate to Dare clothing store. Third prize is tickets to the nature lecture series at the Acorn Falls Natural History Museum."

When she finished reading, the classroom was buzzing. I could tell a lot of the kids were excited about the prizes, and I had to admit, the prizes sounded exciting. I even liked the idea of a nature lecture series. It sounded like a very grown-up thing to do.

Just then Ms. Staats saw my raised hand.

"Yes, Allison," she said, smiling at me.

"Randy Zak, Sabrina Wells, Katie Campbell, and I would like to volunteer as a team," I told her.

"Wonderful," she answered, writing our names down on the sheet of paper in front of her.

"Hey, I want in on this thing, too," said Sam, raising his hand. He looked around. "Who wants to be a team with me?"

"I'll do it with you, dude," said Arizonna Blake.

I wasn't surprised. Arizonna's the kind of person who's really concerned about the world's problems. He just came to Acorn Falls from California a little while ago, but he's definitely into community volunteering.

Nick Robbins and Jason McKee, Sam's best friends, said they'd be on the team, too.

"Very good," said Ms. Staats, writing all of our names down on a sheet of paper.

Lots of other kids in the room had also raised their hands, and I could see that people were inspired to volunteer.

Ten minutes later Ms. Staats had registered all the teams, and homeroom was over.

"Well, class," she said, smiling at us, "I'm very pleased to see that so many of you are interested in getting involved in this project. Now, how you raise the money is, of course, up to you, but I will tell you that the Give-a-Thon deadline is in three weeks, so it would be wise for everyone to start thinking of some ideas."

The bell rang for the end of homeroom. As I gathered up my books, I wondered what Randy, Katie, Sabrina, and I should do to raise our team's money for the Give-a-Thon. I hoped we could think of something really fun to do.

Chapter Two

"This Magic Star thing sounds pretty cool," said Randy as the four of us sat together at Fitzie's later that afternoon. Fitzie's is our favorite place to go after school to eat and to just hang out.

"Really," agreed Sabrina, popping a french fry into her mouth. "I like the idea of a group that goes around granting wishes."

"It's definitely an interesting organization," I said. I took a sip of my soda. "I read an article in the paper about it last week. They help make sick kids' wishes come true, like by taking them to Disney World, or by letting them meet their favorite sports stars."

"That sounds really nice," said Katie, taking a french fry off Sabrina's plate and dipping it in some catsup. "I'm glad we decided to join the Give-a-Thon."

"Yeah," I said, "now all we have to do is figure out how we're going to raise the money."

"I know!" said Sabrina excitedly. "How about a garage sale?"

"I don't think I have much stuff for a garage sale," said Katie. "I think my mother got rid of most of Emily's and my old toys and clothes when we moved."

A little while ago Katie's mother got remarried. Her new stepfather moved Katie and her mother and sister, and her new stepbrother, Michel, to a huge house in a really nice part of Acorn Falls.

"We definitely don't have anything to sell at our house," said Randy. "When M and I came out here from New York, we didn't think we were going to be here very long, so we only brought what M called 'the bare essentials.'"

When Randy and her mother first moved to Acorn Falls, they planned on going back to New York City after a year. But then Randy's mother, who grew up here, decided she wanted to make Acorn Falls her home again. At first Randy was upset about the idea of not moving back to New York, but now she's pretty used to Acorn Falls. As a matter of fact, I sometimes get the feeling that Randy would almost rather stay here instead of going back to New York, although she never actually says so.

"Well, how about a bake sale or something?" suggested Katie. "That's how the girls' basketball team raised the money for their new uniforms."

"Only one problem," I said, grinning. "Who's going to do the baking?"

"Yeah," said Randy. "I mean, it's not like any of the four of us are into cooking or anything."

"I have an idea," I said suddenly. "How about baby-sitting?"

"Ooooh, that sounds fun," said Sabrina excitedly. "I just love little kids."

"Okay by me," said Randy. "It definitely beats baking, anyway."

"We could put up some signs around town to advertise," suggested Katie.

"Great," I said. "We'll put up signs with all our names and phone numbers on them, and anyone who gets a baby-sitting job will save the money for the Give-a-Thon."

"Let's put the signs up this weekend so we can get started right away," said Katie.

"Sounds good to me," I said.

Just then Sam, Nick, Billy Dixon, and Scottie Silver stopped by our table.

I noticed out of the corner of my eye that Katie's cheeks got a little pink. She and Scottie are on Bradley's hockey team together, and they kind of like each other.

"Mmmmm, great! Thanks, Blabs," said Sam, pushing his way into our booth and taking a handful of fries off Sabs's plate. Sam has a habit of calling Sabrina "Blabs," which drives her absolutely crazy.

"Sam, come on!" cried Sabrina, pulling her plate away from him. "Get your own fries."

"Hi, everybody," said Scottie, taking a seat. "Hi, Katie."

"Hi, Scottie," said Katie, smiling.

"So," said Randy, "what are you guys going to do to raise the money?"

Sam looked surprised at my question.

"Who knows?" he said.

"Well, haven't you even thought about it?" asked Sabrina.

Sam looked at Billy and Scottie, and the three of them shrugged.

"Not really," said Scottie.

"We'll come up with something," said Billy. "No problem."

"They say the first prize is a rollerblading

15

party," said Scottie. "Rollerblading's cool — it's a lot like ice-skating. Have you ever tried it, Katie?"

Katie shook her head.

"No, but I'd really like to," she said.

"Sheck says everyone in New York's doing it these days," said Randy.

Sheck was Randy's best friend when she lived in New York. They still keep in touch, and he's even come to Acorn Falls for a visit a few times.

"A rollerblading party would definitely be awesome," said Billy.

"Yeah," said Sam. "But those other prizes — they sounded pretty bogus to me — clothes or something, right?"

"The second prize is not bogus at all," I said quickly. "I would give anything to have a gift certificate to Dare."

"You can say that again!" piped in Sabrina. "I'm telling you guys now, if any of you win the Dare certificate, you *must* give it to me." She gave everyone the eye and then took a sip of her soda. Dare is Sabrina's favorite clothing store. I've gotten a few nice things there, too.

"A certificate to Dare is definitely a great

16

prize," agreed Katie.

"Yeah, some of their clothes are cool," said Sam thoughtfully. "But who would want tickets to the nature lecture series at the Acorn Falls Natural History Museum? Ugh!"

"I thought the third prize sounded kind of boring, too," said Randy.

"Me too," said Scottie. "Who would want to spend a precious day off on a bunch of boring museum lectures?"

"Not me," said Sam. "No way."

"I guess you could always give them to your parents or something if you won them," said Katie.

Actually, I thought the tickets to the nature lecture series sounded kind of fun. I've always been interested in plants and animals. But I didn't say anything.

"Well, I hope we win the rollerblading party," said Scottie. Then he looked at Katie. "Or you do."

"Oh, me too," said Sabrina excitedly. "I've never been to Rob's Rollers, but I've heard it's really nice."

"Well," said Billy, looking at me, "if we win, it's almost like you guys winning, since we would invite you to the party, anyway."

"Hey!" said Sam. "When did we decide that?"

I looked at Billy and smiled.

"If we win, we would definitely invite you guys, too," I said.

"Oh, all right, then," said Sam. "I guess it's a deal."

"Hey, look," said Scottie. "There's Arizonna."

"And there's Jason," said Sam. "Come on. Let's go over and tell them about the 'everybody wins' arrangement we just made."

When the boys had gone, Randy turned to us and said, "Well, they definitely don't seem too worried about how they're going to make their money, do they?"

"Yeah," I agreed, amazed. "Sam said they hadn't even talked about it yet."

"Typical," said Sabrina, shaking her head. "Sam never plans anything ahead."

"You know, it's almost like they've thought more about what it would be like to win than how they're actually going to do it," said Katie.

"That's true," I said. "I mean, it seems like sort of a waste of time to think about the rollerblading party now, when they might not even win."

"Well, that's for sure!" said a familiar voice above me.

I turned to see Stacy Hansen standing by our table, with Eva Malone close behind her.

"Especially since it's pretty obvious whose team is going to win that rollerblading party," Stacy continued, putting her hands on her hips and holding her nose in the air.

"Trust me," added Eva. "No one else has a chance."

"Oh, let me guess, Stacy," said Randy between her teeth. "I'll bet you think you're going to win."

"Wrong, Rowena," said Stacy. "I don't think so. I know so."

I watched Randy turn red with anger. She can't stand Stacy, and she definitely can't stand being called by her real name, Rowena.

"What makes you so sure, Stacy?" Sabrina asked hotly.

"Yes," said Katie, "and do you already have a plan for raising the money?"

"A minor detail," said Stacy, tossing her wavy blond hair. "I'm sure my team will come up with something to do that's worthy of our talents and abilities."

"Oh, I can definitely think of a few things

that would be worthy of *your* talents, Stacy,"
muttered Randy under her breath.

"But I do have a plan worked out for my
rollerblading party," Stacy went on. "It's going
to be the party of the year, right, Eva?"

"Right," said Eva.

"Everybody who's anybody is going to be
there," said Stacy.

"Stacy," I said, "I thought you were joining
the fund-raiser because it's a worthy cause." I
looked at her. "At least, that's what you told Ms.
Staats today in homeroom, wasn't it?"

Stacy put her hands on her hips.

"If you remember, Allison," she said, looking
down at me with a sneer, "I was the first one to
sign up for the Give-a-Thon. Unlike some other
people here who waited until the prizes had
been announced before volunteering."

"That's not fair!" said Sabrina. "We decided
to join before we even knew what the prizes were."

"That's right!" I said angrily. "I had my hand
up, but Ms. Staats didn't call on me until after
she had finished reading the list of prizes."

"Humph," said Stacy. "Sounds pretty suspi-
cious to me."

"Really," said Eva, "that's some story."

"Anyway," Stacy went on, "you might as well give up on the idea of winning right now, because that rollerblading party is mine."

I felt my cheeks burning. Sometimes Stacy can make me so mad.

"Too bad none of you will get to be there," Stacy went on in a sarcastic voice. "I'm just so sorry I won't be able to invite you, but the winning team is allowed to invite only fifty people to the rink, and I'm planning on inviting a lot of eighth graders."

"Yeah," said Eva, sneering. "Too bad."

"Hold on a second, Stacy," I said, looking at my friends. "How did you know that?"

"What?" asked Stacy.

"You just said that the winning team is allowed to invite fifty people to the rollerblading party."

"So?" said Stacy impatiently. "It's true. The winning team, plus fifty guests, at Rob's Rollers. That's the prize. You heard it yourself in homeroom."

"Actually," I said, "that's just the point. I didn't hear how many people could be invited. And neither did anyone else." I looked at her and narrowed my eyes. "It wasn't announced in homeroom."

"Oh, w-wasn't it?" said Stacy, suddenly stammering. "But it must have been . . ."

"No, it wasn't," I said firmly, looking at a page in my notebook. "I wrote down everything Ms. Staats said. Here it is: 'First prize, a rollerblading party at Rob's Rollers.' That's all. So I guess you must have learned the detail about the fifty people from someone else — like maybe your father, the principal!"

Stacy's face turned bright red.

"I don't know what you're talking about!" she said indignantly.

"Which means that you knew about the prizes before the contest was even announced this morning," I went on. "Which is why you volunteered for the Give-a-Thon so quickly."

"Come on, Eva," Stacy said suddenly. "We don't have to stand here and listen to this!"

She turned quickly and stormed away, dragging Eva, who had a slightly puzzled look on her face, behind her.

"Wow, Allie!" said Randy, grinning. "That was amazing!"

"Yeah," said Sabrina. "You really caught her."

"Did you see her face when she realized you

were reading from your notes?" asked Katie, giggling. "I thought she was going to faint."

"Good thing you wrote all that stuff down," said Sabrina.

"Really," said Randy. "Speaking of which, can I borrow a piece of paper, Allie?"

"Sure," I said, tearing a blank sheet out of my notebook. "What do you want it for?"

Randy grinned.

"Well, I was just thinking," she said. "I mean, look what you just managed to accomplish with your notes."

"So?" I said. "I still don't get it."

"So, maybe there's more to this note-taking stuff than I thought." She took the piece of paper from me and grinned. "From now on, I want to take notes everywhere I go!"

I looked at Randy, then I looked at Sabrina and Katie. Suddenly we all burst out laughing. I tore another page out of my notebook, balled it up, and threw it right at Rowena Zak!

Chapter Three

"Okay," I said, looking down at the thick textbook in front of me. "What's 'territorial behavior'?"

It was Thursday afternoon and I was in Mary's room, on the second floor of our house, helping her study for the big psychology exam she had coming up.

"Territorial behavior is wanting to keep strangers out of your home area," Mary answered. "Like, when a lion fights against another lion who is trying to intrude on the land where his family lives. Humans do it, too, by building fences around their property. And when two countries fight a war over a piece of land that they both think they own, that's a major example of humans being territorial."

I nodded. It seemed to make sense to me.

I was sitting in Mary's desk chair, with her psychology book open in front of me. She and my little brother, Charlie, were lying on their stomachs on the floor, working on a giant jig-saw puzzle of a bunch of zebras running across a field. There were hundreds of tiny black-and-white-striped puzzle pieces all over the floor, and Charlie's new puppy, Ralph, kept trying to pick them up in his mouth. I couldn't imagine how Mary was managing to concentrate on helping Charlie with the puzzle, keeping the pieces away from Ralph, and answering the questions I was asking her, all at the same time.

"Okay," I said, flipping my braid over my shoulder as I read the next question, "what's 'conditioning'?"

"Conditioning is when somebody learns to do something by getting rewarded for it," said Mary. Her silver bracelets jingled as she grabbed a puzzle piece from Ralph and pushed it into place. "It can be anything from a dog learning to sit and roll over because you give it a treat, to a kid learning to put his toys away because you praise him for doing it."

I nodded.

"I put my toys away," said Charlie, looking up suddenly from the puzzle. "Sometimes."

"'Sometimes' is right," said Mary, grinning.

I laughed. Charlie is not exactly neat. In fact,

his room is usually pretty much of a mess. I wonder how the two of us can even be related. It doesn't seem to bother Charlie at all to have piles of toy soldiers, yo-yos, baseballs, and dirty socks all over the place.

I continued down the list of questions, reading them out loud to Mary, until I heard my grandmother call us for dinner. Both of my grandparents live with us, in their own little apartment attached to the back of our house, and my grandmother does a lot of the cooking for our family, especially now that my mother has my baby sister to take care of.

"Yeah, dinner!" said Charlie, jumping up from the floor. "Come on, Ralphie, let's go downstairs."

He ran out the door and down the hall, with Ralph bounding behind him.

"Charlie! Don't forget," Mary called after him, "Ralph stays on the floor, not at the table!"

She looked at me and shook her head.

"Why do I get the feeling that when we get down there, he'll have that dog on his lap again?" she asked.

"Maybe because he tries it every night?" I said, grinning at her.

Ralph has only been with us for a little while. Charlie and I went to the Acorn Falls Animal Shelter recently to pick him out. At first Ralph's behavior was pretty wild. He ran around a lot, made a lot of noise, and chewed things he wasn't supposed to, like my father's slippers. I'm pretty sure that was because he had been locked up in a cage for so long. Actually, it turned out that conditions for a lot of the animals at the shelter were pretty bad, so my friends and I started a campaign to get the animals adopted. It was called Pick-a-Pet Day. Thanks to a lot of help from the kids at Bradley, some Acorn Falls store owners, and a few other people in the community, it was a success.

Lately the whole family has been doing their best to train Ralph not to chew things and not to beg at the table. But sometimes it's hard to get Charlie to help. He's crazy about Ralph and really hates saying no to him for any reason.

Sure enough, when Mary and I got down to the dining room, Ralph was perched on Charlie's lap. My grandfather, who was sitting on the other side of the table, hadn't even noticed.

"Well, hello, there, young ladies. Glad to see

you," said my grandfather. "I was beginning to think it was just going to be me and Charlie for dinner."

"Not exactly," I muttered to Mary, looking over at Ralph's wagging tail, which was sticking out from under the tablecloth above Charlie's legs.

Charlie saw me notice Ralph and gave me a pleading look.

"Come on, Charlie. Remember our deal," said Mary.

"Oh, okay," said Charlie, pushing his chair back and letting Ralph down to the floor.

"Deal?" I asked, looking at Mary and raising my eyebrows.

"That's right," she said. "You see, Charlie and I have this project we've been working on lately — it's called 'Teaching Ralph That He's a Dog.'"

I grinned. It was true that Charlie tended to treat Ralph more like a person than a dog, like wanting to let him sit at the table and sleep in his bed. Somehow, I had the feeling that Mary's "project" was more about teaching *Charlie* that Ralph was a dog than teaching Ralph about it.

"So," Mary went on, smiling, "every time

Charlie remembers to treat Ralph like a dog, he and I take Ralph out to have some fun like a dog."

"We go outside with him and run around the house ten times," added Charlie excitedly. "Ralph loves it."

"Well, that sounds like a regular barrel of monkeys," said my grandfather, smiling. "Maybe sometime I'll join you."

I shook my head. I couldn't exactly imagine my grandfather out running around the house, but there was no doubt in my mind that Mary definitely knew what to do when it came to handling Charlie. Suddenly I had a thought. Maybe this was a little bit like that "conditioning" stuff that Mary had explained to me — teaching someone to do something by rewarding them for it. Running around the house with Ralph and Mary was Charlie's reward for learning to treat Ralph like a dog.

Just then my grandmother walked in.

"You're not keeping that dog at the table again, are you, young man?" she asked, putting a platter of chicken on the table.

"No, Nooma," said Charlie with a smile.

Nooma is what my whole family calls my

grandmother. It comes from the Chippewa word for "grandmother."

"Well, hello, everyone," said my mother, coming into the dining room with my baby sister, Barrett, on her hip. "Where's Nathan?" she asked, putting Barrett in her high chair and looking around for my father. "Didn't he hear us call?"

"Probably still working," said my grandmother, passing Mary the peas. "Seems that man is always working."

"I'll get him," I said, pushing back my chair and standing up.

I knew my father was probably in his study in the back of our house. His study used to be on the second floor, but when Mary came to live with us a little while ago, we turned that room into her bedroom and moved his study down to a room we used to use for storage.

My father spends a lot of time in his study. He's a lawyer, and he works long hours at his office in town. But it seems like he always has work to bring home at night, too. I guess it's because he takes on cases of people who can't afford to hire a lawyer.

"Dad," I said, knocking on the door to his

study. "Dad, it's time for dinner."

"Okay, be there in a minute," he mumbled.

I opened the door and saw him hunched over the computer at his desk.

"Dad," I said. "Come on. Everybody's at the table."

He looked up from his work and grinned sheepishly.

"Oh, hi, Allison," he said. "Here I come. I guess I've been saying 'just a minute' for the past fifteen minutes, haven't I?"

I smiled at him. I know what it's like to be really involved in what you're doing. I get that way sometimes, too, when I'm working on something I'm really interested in, like writing a poem or reading.

"Well, there you are!" said my mother with a smile as my father and I walked into the dining room.

"Sorry to keep you waiting, Meredith," said my father, bending down to give my mother a kiss before taking his place at the table.

"You shouldn't spend so long in front of that computer," said my grandmother, passing my father the platter of chicken. "You'll ruin your eyes."

"Don't worry about me, Nooma," said my father. He took a piece of chicken and put it on his plate.

"You have been working awfully long hours lately, Nathan," said my mother, buttering a piece of my grandmother's homemade corn bread.

"Well, I've got a big case coming up," said my father. "I'm defending a man accused of shooting another man."

"Oh, Nathan, how awful," said my mother.

"Yes, well, but the man had broken into my client's house and was trying to rob him," my father explained.

"I suppose that does make it a little more understandable," said my mother. "Although it's still a terrible thing to have happen."

"My client was just trying to protect his family and his home," my father said. "He did what he had to under the circumstances. Now all I have to do is convince a jury of that."

Suddenly I had a thought — what my father was talking about sounded a lot like that "territorial behavior" stuff in Mary's psychology book. After all, hadn't she said that it meant trying to keep strangers from intruding into your home area? That sounded like what my father's client had done. This psychology stuff was beginning to seem like it could fit in just about everywhere.

"Enough about my work, though," said my father, giving us all a big smile. "One of the reasons I enjoy sitting down with my family at night is that I can forget about work."

"Oh, I almost forgot," Nooma said. "I got a letter from Sally Little Bear. You remember Sally and John Little Bear — they lived next door to us on the reservation when you were growing up, Nathan."

"Sure," said my father, "I remember them well. You and Mrs. Little Bear were good friends. They moved to California, didn't they?"

"That's right," said my grandfather. "They moved to San Diego. They said they wanted to feel the sunshine every day."

"Well, they must miss spring in Minnesota, after all," said my grandmother, "because they're coming back for a visit. They have relatives on the reservation, and they're going to be staying there for a while. Grandpa and I thought we might go to see them."

"That sounds like a lovely idea, Nooma," said my mother. "When will they be there?"

"They arrive next weekend, and we thought we'd go out for a week or so," answered my grandmother. "But are you sure you can manage everything here without us? I mean, with the children and all?"

"We'll be fine, Nooma," said my mother. "Not that we don't depend on you for a lot. But I think we can survive for a week on our own."

"Sure," said my father. "It'll do you both some good to get away for a little while. Besides, we've got Mary to help us out. And I'm sure Allison can pitch in and help take care of Charlie and the baby, too."

"Fine," I said, nodding. "I'll be glad to help."

"Oh," said Mary suddenly. "I've got my study group on Friday nights, though. For my psychology exam. Is it still okay if I go, or do you need me to stay home?"

"No, you go right ahead, Mary," said my mother.

"That's right," said my father. "Now that's what I like to see — a student who actually studies on a Friday night."

Mary's face flushed.

"Well, actually, Mr. Cloud, that was just the only night that all of us in the group have free," she explained. "You see, this exam's a really big one. It counts for half of our grade for the term. So a bunch of us in the class decided to get together every week to study for it together."

"Well, I still think it's very commendable," said my father. "A good education is one of the most important things in life. Speaking of which, how's school going for you two these days, Charlie and Allison? Anything new?"

"Patrick Cunningham threw up today," Charlie volunteered.

"Oh, Charlie," said my mother. "Not at the dinner table, please."

"No, it was at the lunch table," Charlie said.

I giggled, realizing that Charlie had misunderstood what my mother had said.

"You see," Charlie went on, "Mrs. Brodman tried to make him eat macaroni and cheese, and Patrick said he hated macaroni and cheese, and —"

"That's enough, Charlie," said Nooma sharply.

"Well, Mr. Hansen made an interesting announcement in school yesterday," I said quickly, trying to change the subject. "Bradley's going to join the annual Give-a-Thon for the Magic Star Foundation."

"The Magic Star Foundation," my mother said. "Isn't that the group that works with sick children?"

"That's right," I said, helping myself to more rice. "They help grant the kids' wishes. And they're sponsoring a contest at Bradley to see who can raise the most money for their Give-a-Thon. There are prizes and everything."

"That's a very clever idea," said my father, spearing some string beans with his fork. "Getting kids involved through a contest. Are you going to enter, Allison?"

"Actually, there are competing teams," I explained. "And yes, Randy, Katie, Sabrina, and I formed a team. We have three weeks to raise the money."

"Have you decided how you're going to do it?" asked my mother.

"We thought we might try baby-sitting," I said. "We're going to put some signs up around Acorn Falls, and anytime one of us gets a baby-sitting job, we'll save the money for the Give-a-Thon."

"That sounds like a good idea," said my mother. "You know, there's a big bulletin board at the supermarket. You might want to put a sign there, since a lot of mothers do their shopping there."

"Thanks, Mom," I said. "That's a good idea."

"There's a wall down at the Knitting Needle where people put up advertisements, too," suggested my grandmother. "I always notice it when I go in to buy yarn."

"That's a good idea, too, Nooma," I said. "In fact, I bet there are lots of stores in town where we could advertise."

Suddenly I felt very excited. I had never really had a real, paying baby-sitting job before, and I couldn't wait to put those signs up on Saturday so I could get my first job.

Chapter Four

WE CARE FOR KIDS!
FOUR RESPONSIBLE, SENSITIVE 7TH GRADERS
AVAILABLE FOR BABY-SITTING. FEES WILL BE
DONATED TO A GOOD CAUSE.

"There," said Sabrina, standing back and putting her hands in the pockets of her oversize green sweatshirt. "That ought to get noticed."

I looked at the sign, one of several that Randy had designed with big black lettering on bright orange–colored paper. Sabs, Katie, Randy, and I had listed our phone numbers on the bottom of each piece of paper.

"It definitely stands out," I agreed.

It was Saturday, and the four of us were standing in front of the bulletin board at the supermarket, where my mother had suggested we put one of our baby-sitting signs.

"Come on," I said. "The Knitting Needle is

just down the street. My grandmother says they have a place for ads there, too."

"Hey," said Randy suddenly, "I think there's a bulletin board over at Sal's Sounds, the music store. Mostly it's just people trying to sell used instruments and stuff, though."

"Well, it probably couldn't hurt to put one up there, anyway," said Katie.

"Definitely," I said. "I mean, musicians have kids, too, right?"

"Sounds good to me," said Randy. "I kind of need to pick up a new set of sticks, anyway."

Randy's a great drummer. She's really serious about it, too. She plays with this band called Iron Wombat. I don't know that much about rock music, but to me Randy's band sounds just as good as anything I hear on the radio.

"Okay, then," I said, tossing my ponytail over my shoulder and buttoning my blue quilted jacket. "Let's go."

A half hour later we had put up signs in Sal's Sounds, the Knitting Needle, Fun Time Toys, and Andersen's Bakery.

"Okay," I said as we came out of the bakery, "now all we have left is the Acorn Falls Community Library and the YMCA."

"Before we do that, let's stop in at the sporting goods store," suggested Katie. "It's right across the street, and I think they have a bulletin board there. I'm pretty sure I noticed one the last time I went in to have my skates sharpened."

"That's a good idea," I agreed. "Lots of people with kids shop there."

The four of us walked across the street to Sports World. Katie pulled open one of the big glass doors, and we followed her in.

The store was unbelievably crowded. We almost bumped smack into Scottie Silver, who was hurrying by with a big stack of what looked like oversize shoe boxes.

"Hey, excuse me!" shouted Scottie, struggling to keep the stack of boxes balanced in his arms. He looked at us again, and his face softened. "Katie, hi! Sorry, I didn't realize that was you." He looked at the rest of us and grinned. "Welcome to Sports World, everybody. What can I do for you today?"

"Scottie, you're kidding!" Katie burst out, amazed. "You're working here now?"

"Cool," said Randy. "How long have you been doing this?"

Scottie grinned.

"Actually, it's just for the big sale today," he told us. "I'm too young to have a regular job here."

"But how did you get the job?" asked Katie.

"Well, I came in to look at some hockey sticks," he answered. "I had heard they were having the sale, and I thought I might get a new one. When Mark, the manager, saw me, he asked me if I wanted to help out. You see, he knows me really well, because I come in all the time, so he knows I know a lot about skating. So he asked me to work in the skate department for the day. He said he'd pay me thirty-five dollars."

"Thirty-five dollars!" said Sabrina, her hazel eyes lighting up.

"Pretty good, huh?" said Scottie. "I figure I'll give it to my team for the Give-a-Thon Contest." He looked around. "Listen, I gotta go. There are a bunch of people waiting to try on skates on the other side of the store. See you in school on Monday, Katie."

He hurried off in the other direction, the stack of boxes swaying in his arms.

"Wow," said Randy, shaking her head. "That's some gig — thirty-five dollars for one day."

"That means the boys' team is already way ahead of us," said Sabrina, sighing.

"I guess we should be glad that Scottie has the chance to earn that much money for Magic Star," said Katie. "But it still does kind of bother me that I could have done that job. I mean, I know as much about skates as Scottie does."

"Well, I guess Scottie was just in the right place at the right time," I said. "Besides, I'm sure we'll all start to get lots of job offers once people notice our baby-sitting ads."

"Allie's right," said Sabrina. "Scottie was just really lucky. Soon we'll make some money, too."

"Speaking of which, when we finish putting up our sign here, let's go over to the library and the Y and put up the other signs," suggested Randy.

"Good idea," I said. "Then maybe we can head over to Fitzie's for some sodas and fries."

The library and the YWCA are on the other side of downtown Acorn Falls, so it took us about ten minutes to walk there. We put the sign up at the Y first, and then headed over to the library.

As we stood in front of the library bulletin board, I noticed another brightly colored flier. It read:

ANNOUNCING
THE BRADLEY JUNIOR HIGH
SEVENTH-GRADE CAR-WASH TEAM
MARATHON CAR WASH.
ONE DAY ONLY!!!
WE WASH BY HAND & DO A GREAT JOB!
ONLY $5 A CAR.
DON'T MISS IT!
ALL MONEY COLLECTED
WILL GO TO CHARITY.

"Wow," I said, pointing at the sign. "Look at that."

"It must be another one of the Bradley Give-a-Thon teams," said Katie. "I wonder whose it is."

"A car wash, that sounds like fun," said Sabrina. "Maybe we should do that instead."

"It probably wouldn't be such a good idea," I said. "I mean, since another team is already doing it."

"That's true," said Sabs.

"How much money can they make if they only charge five dollars a car?" Randy asked.

"It depends how many people show up, I

guess," said Katie.

"They could do pretty well if they got enough business," I said. "And they do only have to work for one day."

"I guess they came up with a pretty good idea," said Katie.

"Speaking of good ideas," said Sabrina, "how about going over to Fitzie's for those sodas and fries now? I'm bushed."

"That sounds great," said Katie.

"Definitely," I agreed.

"Hey!" Sabrina said suddenly, looking across the street. "Doesn't that look like Sam over there?" She pointed at a guy working on the lawn of a house.

"It sure does!" said Randy.

"It is Sam, isn't it?" I said, squinting.

"No way," said Sabrina. "Not my brother. That guy's trimming the hedge around that house. Sam hardly does any work around *our* yard. He definitely wouldn't be working in someone else's."

"Are you sure?" said Katie. "I mean, it really looks like him."

"Really," said Randy. "There are only two people in Acorn Falls with that color of red hair,

Sabs. You're one of them, and Sam is the other."

Suddenly another guy came walking around from the back of the house, his arms full of dead branches. I recognized him right away.

"That *must* be Sam," I said, "because there's Billy Dixon!"

"Ohmygosh! You're right!" said Sabrina. "Come on. Let's go find out what they're doing."

We hurried across the street to the house, where Sam was still trimming the hedges and Billy was adding the dead branches to a big pile of others.

Billy's face lit up when he saw us.

"Hi, Allison. Hi, guys!" he said, standing up and wiping his hands off on his worn jeans.

"Hi, Billy," I said, still surprised to see him.

"Blabs, what are you doing here?" asked Sam, looking up from the hedge in amazement.

"*I'm* the one who should ask you that, Sam!" said Sabrina, putting her hands on her hips.

"We're working," said Billy, grinning proudly. "Isn't it cool? Sam and I are going to be the first ones on our team to raise some money for the contest."

"Wait till we tell the other guys," said Sam happily. "This puts us ten dollars closer to winning that rollerblading party."

"First of all, you're not the first ones on your team to get a job," said Sabrina.

"Huh?" said Sam.

"Scottie's working down at Sports World for the day," Katie explained.

"Great!" said Billy. "I mean, every little bit helps, right?"

The thirty-five dollars that Scottie had said he was earning by working at Sports World hardly seemed like a "little bit" to me, but I didn't say anything.

"And second of all," Sabrina continued, "how did you guys get this job?"

"Did you put ads up or something?" I asked. "We've been to practically every bulletin board in town, and we haven't seen anything advertising yard work."

"Nah, we weren't even looking for this," Sam said. "Actually, Billy and I were heading over to the basketball courts behind the high school to shoot some hoops."

"We passed by this house, and there was a lady outside who asked us if we wanted to help her out with her yard for the day," explained Billy. "So we figured, why not?"

"We'd better get back to work, though, if we want to get finished in time to make it to the courts and play some ball while it's still light out," said Sam.

"Okay, Sam," said Billy. "Why don't you come around back and help me get the rest of these branches?" He looked at me and smiled, his blue eyes twinkling. "I'm really glad we ran into you guys," he said. "I guess I'll see you on Monday, Allison."

"Bye, Billy," I said. "Have a good time playing basketball."

"Wow," said Randy as the four of us headed down the street together toward Fitzie's. "Can you beat that?"

"Really!" said Sabs hotly. "It's only four days into the contest, and Sam's team has already made forty-five dollars!"

"The really incredible thing is that Scottie, Sam, and Billy weren't even looking for work," I said, shaking my head in amazement.

"I know," said Katie. "It's like those jobs just fell into their laps!"

"Gee, I don't know," I said, grinning suddenly. "Are you guys sure you still want to go to Fitzie's?"

"Of course!" said Sabrina.

"Why wouldn't we want to go?" asked Katie.

"Well," I said, breaking into a smile, "the way things are going for the boys' team, I can't help getting the feeling that when we get there, Nick, Jason, and Arizonna will turn out to be our waiters!"

We all burst out laughing. Somehow, the idea of Nick, Jason, and Arizonna running around Fitzie's with aprons on, taking orders and serving up fries and ice cream, struck us as really funny. By the time we walked into Fitzie's, we were laughing so hard we had tears running down our cheeks.

Chapter Five

Sabrina calls Katie.

MICHEL: Hello?

SABRINA: Hi, Michel, it's me, Sabs.

MICHEL: Oh, hello, Sabrina. How are you?

SABRINA: I'm fine, thanks, Michel. Is Katie there?

MICHEL: No, I'm sorry. She went out.

SABRINA: Out? Where did she go?

MICHEL: I think she said she had to go to a baby-sitting job.

SABRINA: Baby-sitting?! That's great, Michel. Listen, can you tell her I called when she gets back?

MICHEL: Yes, Sabrina. I will leave her a note.

SABRINA: Thanks, Michel. Bye.

Sabrina calls Allison.

MARY: Hello, Cloud residence. Mary Birdsong speaking.

SABRINA: Hi, Mary. This is Sabrina. Is Allison there?

MARY: Sure, she's just down the hall in my room. I'll get her. (*A moment later . . .*)

ALLISON: Hi, Sabs. What's up?

SABRINA: Hi, Allison. Guess what? I just called Katie's house, and she's not there.

ALLISON: Oh, great. Did she get a baby-sitting job?

SABRINA: How did you know?

ALLISON: I just had a hunch. Anyway, it's great that Katie got a job. Do you know who it's for, or how old the kids are, or anything?

SABRINA: No, I haven't talked to her. She must have gotten the call about it pretty recently. Thank goodness one of us finally got called, though. I was beginning to think we weren't going to be able to raise any money for the Give-a-Thon!

ALLISON: I know. It's been over a week since we put those signs up, and none of us has had a baby-sitting offer until now. I'm starting to wonder if this is going to work.

SABRINA: You mean, you think baby-sitting is a bad idea?

ALLISON: Well, baby-sitting might not be the problem, but the way we are going about it might be. I mean, we just put up a bunch of signs and sat back and waited for the jobs to find us.

SABRINA: Well, jobs sure seem to find the guys on my brother's team easily enough! Do you know that when Billy and Sam finished that lady's yard, her neighbor offered to hire them the next day to do his yard?

ALLISON: The guys have definitely been lucky.

SABRINA: And not only that, but then my father offered to pay them to clean out the garage! I couldn't believe it — now they're getting all the jobs at my house, too! Wait till you hear their next plan, though. They're holding a bake sale at lunch the day after tomorrow in the school cafeteria.

ALLISON: You're kidding! Don't tell me that Sam and Billy and those guys are actually going to bake?!

SABRINA: No, that's just it — they're planning on selling store-bought stuff.

ALLISON: That sounds pretty weird. I mean, isn't the whole idea of a bake sale to sell homemade stuff that people can't get in stores?

SABRINA: That's what I said. But of course they won't listen to me. I can just see it now — Sam and his team in the cafeteria trying to sell slices of frozen pound cake and cookies from a box. I'll be embarrassed in front of the whole school.

ALLISON: (*Giggling*) It is sort of funny, if you think about it. Listen, Sabs, I've got to go. Call me back if you get any news from Katie.

SABRINA: Okay, Allie. Bye.

Katie calls Sabrina.

SABRINA: Hello?

KATIE: Hi, Sabs, it's me. Guess where I am?

SABRINA: Um, baby-sitting?

KATIE: Hey, how did you know that?

SABRINA: Well, I just thought logically. You see, I knew you weren't with any of your friends, and that meant you were probably doing something else, like working. (*Laughs*) Just kidding, Katie. Actually, Michel told me.

KATIE: Oh, good. I wanted to call you and tell you about it, but the mother said she needed me to come over right away, so I didn't get a chance.

SABRINA: So how is it? What are the kids like?

KATIE: Actually, it's really easy. It's a little baby, and he's been sleeping the whole time, so there hasn't .really been anything for me to do. I did my homework, watched some TV, and decided to call you.

SABRINA: Well, it sounds like a pretty easy

way to earn money, at least.

KATIE: I guess so, but the parents are going to be back soon, so I don't think I'll make that much.

SABRINA: Gee, I guess it's going to take a lot of baby-sitting if we want to catch up with the boys' team.

KATIE: Are they still getting jobs handed to them all over the place?

SABRINA: That's for sure. The other day my father even hired them to do something.

KATIE: Well, that doesn't seem very fair, Sabs.

SABRINA: Hey, I guess you're right.

KATIE: I mean, you and Sam are both competing in the same contest, right? Your parents shouldn't be helping one of you out and not the other.

SABRINA: You're totally right, Katie. I didn't think of it that way. I think I'll complain to my mom.

KATIE: I should get off the phone, anyway, Sabs.

SABRINA: Okay, Katie. Thanks for calling. Have fun baby-sitting.

KATIE: Okay, Sabs. Bye.

A little while later, Sabrina calls Allison back.

ALLISON: Hello?

SABRINA: Hi, Allie. It's me again.

ALLISON: Oh, hi, Sabs.

SABRINA: Listen, I just wanted to let you know that I talked to Katie. She called me from her baby-sitting job. She says it's really easy, just a baby that's been asleep the whole time. She also said that she thought it was unfair of my parents to give Sam's team a job and not give us one — that it was kind of like helping Sam in the contest and not helping me.

ALLISON: That's a good point.

SABRINA: I thought so, too. So I talked to my mother about it. She says she's willing to hire the four of us to clean the attic if we want. She'll pay us ten dollars, which is how much my father paid Sam's team to do the garage.

ALLISON: Fine with me. When should we

do it?

SABRINA: How about tomorrow after school?

ALLISON: Okay, I'll call Randy and tell her about it.

SABRINA: And I'll try Katie a little later. She should be home from baby-sitting in a while.

ALLISON: Okay, Sabs, see you tomorrow.

SABRINA: Bye, Allie.

Allison calls Randy.

ALLISON: Hi, Randy, it's me, Allie.

RANDY: Hi, Allie, what's new?

ALLISON: Actually, two things. First of all, Katie got a baby-sitting job.

RANDY: Wow, cool. Hey, it's about time one of us got a call from all those fliers we put up.

ALLISON: I know. Sabs did find us another job, though, if you want to do it. It's cleaning out the attic at her house. Her mother's willing to pay us ten dollars to do it.

RANDY: Sounds good to me.

ALLISON: Great. We thought we'd do it

tomorrow after school.

RANDY: Fine.

ALLISON: Okay, see you tomorrow then.

RANDY: Okay, Allison. *Ciao*.

Chapter Six

"Wow, look at all this stuff!" said Randy as the four of us stood in the Wellses' storage attic the next day after school.

I looked around at the piles of boxes that were stacked all over the room.

"Gee, I can't believe how much stuff we keep putting up here," said Sabrina. She bent down to run her finger through the inch-deep dust on the floor. "No wonder my mother wants this place cleaned up and organized."

"Good thing we all wore old clothes," I said, looking down at my faded jeans and red-and-black-checkered flannel shirt.

"I guess we'd better get started," said Katie, pulling her hair into a pink scrunchie. "This looks like it might be a pretty big job."

"But where do we start?" asked Sabrina, looking around.

"I guess we have to move all the boxes out

first so we can dust and sweep up this dirt," I said.

"Okay," said Randy, lifting up one of the boxes, "here goes."

Moving the boxes turned out to be a really big job. The Wellses' attic is divided into two sides. One side is used for storage, and the other side is Sabrina's bedroom. It would have been easier if we could have just moved all the boxes into Sabs's half of the attic while we were cleaning. But, unfortunately, there isn't any door connecting the storage half to her half. That meant we had to lower all the boxes down out of the attic by the steep stairs that lead to the floor below.

After a few minutes we figured out a system. Sabs would bring a box over to me at the top of the stairs, and I would hand it to Katie, who was standing halfway down the stairs. Then she would give it to Randy, who was at the bottom. This made things move a little faster. But it was still really hard work. By the time we had finished moving all the boxes, about an hour later, we were pretty tired.

"Phew," sighed Sabrina, sitting down on one of the boxes and blowing a lock of her curly auburn hair off her forehead. "That was exhausting!"

"It sure was," agreed Katie, wiping her forehead with the back of her hand.

"And we still have to dust, sweep, and mop," I pointed out, sighing.

"And then dust all those boxes and put them back up there," groaned Katie.

"What's in all these boxes, anyway?" said Randy, reaching over to pull the lid off one.

A cloud of dust came flying out.

"Agh!" she said, coughing and fanning away the dust. Sabs looked into the box. "Wow! Look at this!"

Standing up, she pulled out a long cream-colored dress with little yellow roses all over it.

"That's beautiful, Sabs," I said, reaching out to touch the satiny fabric.

"It must have been my mother's," she replied, holding it up and looking at it.

"It looks like a prom dress or something," said Katie.

"I think you're right, Katie," agreed Randy, reaching into the box and pulling out an old photograph in a frame.

"Ooooh, look," squealed Sabs, taking the

photo from Randy. "It's my mom and dad on their prom night."

I looked at the picture. There were two much younger versions of Sabrina's parents, standing at the foot of a staircase. Sabrina's father was wearing a tuxedo, and her mother was wearing the dress with the yellow flowers. Tied to her wrist was a white corsage.

"Wow," I said, "your mother kind of looks like you in that picture, Sabs."

"You think so?" asked Sabrina, squinting at the picture.

"Definitely," said Katie.

"I wonder if this dress would fit me," said Sabs. "Maybe I'll take it up to my room when we put the boxes back. I kind of like the picture, too. It might look neat on top of my dresser."

"Maybe we should take a little break before we start sweeping," suggested Randy. "I'm totaled."

"Good idea," agreed Sabrina. "Let's go downstairs and get a snack or something. We have to go down to the kitchen to get the brooms and dustpans and stuff, anyway."

When we got downstairs, we found Sam,

Nick, and Jason sitting at the kitchen table. In front of them were several packages of cake, cookies, and brownies.

"Oh, good," said Sabrina, reaching for a bag of chocolate chip cookies. "Looks like Mom bought some yummy stuff."

"Hey!" said Sam, snatching the bag from her. "Mom didn't buy that. This stuff is for our bake sale tomorrow."

"Yeah," cracked Jason. "Keep your paws off."

"Bake sale?" said Katie. "But these are store-bought cookies."

"Oh, didn't I tell you?" said Sabrina. "This is Sam's latest brilliant idea — the store-bought bake sale."

"Hey, don't knock it," said Nick.

"Really," said Sam, "you were pretty excited about eating these 'store-bought' cookies when you first walked in the kitchen, if I remember, Sabs."

"That's because we're totally exhausted and starving, Sam," said Randy.

"We've been upstairs cleaning the attic for an hour," I explained.

"Come on, Sam," said Sabrina. "Just let us

have a couple of cookies."

Sam looked at Nick and Jason.

"Well," he said, grinning, "all right. But it's going to cost you."

"Cost us?!" exclaimed Sabrina. "Sam Wells, I am not going to pay to eat cookies in my own house!"

"But these are bake sale cookies," said Sam. "I have to charge you. I mean, it wouldn't be very fair for us to give these cookies out to you guys for free when we're going to be charging twenty-five cents apiece for them tomorrow, would it?"

A few minutes later we walked out of the kitchen with eight cookies and four glasses of milk.

"At least the milk was free," muttered Sabrina.

"I can't believe we actually just contributed two dollars to the boys' team," I said with a big sigh.

"Believe me, it'll probably be the only money they make off that silly bake sale," said Katie.

"You bet," said Randy. "Who ever heard of selling store-bought cookies for twenty-five cents each?"

After we had finished our snack, we trudged back up to the attic with the brooms, dustpans, and mops. The attic must not have been cleaned in years. It took another hour just to sweep the place, and once we started mopping, the bucket of water got so dirty we had to change it every five minutes. By the time we had finished cleaning, and carrying all the boxes back up into the attic, we were completely exhausted and covered with dirt and grime.

"Ohmygosh," said Sabrina, looking around the attic. "Are we actually finished?"

"Finally." Randy sighed, wiping her forehead with the back of her hand. "I feel like we've been doing this for hours."

"We have been doing it for hours," I said, looking down at my watch. "Three hours, to be exact."

"Three hours?!" exclaimed Katie. "I'd better call home to see if someone can come pick me up. Do you want a ride home, Randy and Allison?"

"Yep," said Randy.

"Sure, Katie, thanks," I said, thinking of all the homework I still had to get done that night.

"Well, at least we can add ten dollars to our

Give-a-Thon kitty," said Sabrina.

"You know," said Randy, "that's a pretty decent amount of money to earn in one afternoon."

I thought for a moment.

"I hate to be the one to point this out," I said, "but that's ten dollars earned by four people. Which means we each only earned two dollars and fifty cents."

"Ugh," said Sabrina. "Only two-fifty each for all that work. How much is that an hour, Allison?"

"About eighty-three cents," I admitted.

"Gee," said Katie, "we were better off baby-sitting."

"Except most of us didn't even get to do any baby-sitting," said Randy glumly.

"Oh, well," I said. "I'm sure something will come up. And at least we made some money today. That's better than nothing, right?"

But even as I spoke, I couldn't help feeling like we were so far behind in the Give-a-Thon Contest, we might never catch up.

"Come and get them! Come and get them!" Sam called out loudly.

"Sorry, dude, we're all out of the brownies," I heard Arizonna say. "How about a couple of these peanut butter cookies instead? They're only twenty-five cents, and the money goes to a good cause."

It was the next day in school, and Sabrina, Randy, Katie, and I were standing in the cafeteria, looking over at the table where the boys were holding their bake sale.

"Can you believe this?" said Sabrina, staring at the crowd of kids surrounding the table.

"I never would have thought it could happen," said Katie, shaking her head. "They're doing tons of business."

"I guess kids will pay anything for something sweet at lunchtime," said Randy, sighing, "even if it does come from a package."

"I suppose even store-bought tastes better than the stuff they serve here in the cafeteria," I admitted. "That must be why they're doing so much business."

"If only we had known," moaned Sabrina, "then we could have done this."

"You're right," agreed Katie. "Selling cookies sure would beat cleaning attics to raise money for the Give-a-Thon."

"Ick!" said a voice behind us. "Cleaning attics — what a disgusting-sounding thing to do!"

I turned around to see Stacy, Eva, B.Z., and Laurel standing behind us. Stacy was chewing on a giant brownie from the bake sale.

"Our team would certainly never stoop that low, would we?" Stacy went on, taking another bite of her brownie.

"Certainly not!" huffed Eva.

"How gross," commented B.Z.

Suddenly I felt my cheeks burning. I had had just about all I could take of Stacy and her snobby attitude.

"You know, Stacy, there's nothing wrong with getting your hands a little dirty for a good cause!" I blurted out.

"Well," said Stacy, lifting her nose higher in the air, "maybe for *your* team. Although I must admit, I am a little surprised at you, Katie Campbell. I thought you had servants to do that kind of thing for you now."

I saw Katie's face turn red.

"I'm just thankful none of us will ever have to do anything that lowly for the contest," Stacy went on.

"And what do you guys plan to do then, get paid for sitting around and looking good?" asked Randy snidely.

"Actually, you're very close, Rowena," Stacy sneered back. "It just so happens that my team has been hired to be hostesses at the next Ladies' Garden Club luncheon. They want a few refined, attractive young ladies to greet guests at the door and show them to their seats." She stuffed the last of her brownie into her mouth.

"Well, then why'd they hire you guys?" Randy asked innocently.

I put my hand over my mouth to stifle a giggle.

Stacy's face turned red. She opened her mouth to yell something back, but her cheeks were still filled with brownie, and all that came out was a spray of brown crumbs.

"Stacy, I'm surprised at you," said Katie, holding back her laughter. "I thought you were refined enough to know better than to talk with your mouth full like that."

Still holding in our giggles, we hurried away, leaving Eva, B.Z., and Laurel with their mouths hanging open, and Stacy struggling with her brownie.

"Katie, you sure told her," said Sabrina.

"Stacy is such a snob," I said. "I wonder if she was telling the truth about that hostessing job, though."

"I'm pretty sure she was," said Katie. "You see, Laurel Spencer's mother is the president of the Acorn Falls Ladies' Garden Club. I know because when we first moved to our new house, Mrs. Spencer sent my mother an invitation to join. My mom sent back this really fancy-looking note saying that since the Ladies' Garden Club hadn't been interested in her for all the years she had lived in Acorn Falls before she had moved to a big house, she certainly wasn't interested in them now."

"Wow, that's great," said Randy. "Your mom's pretty cool, Katie."

"I guess Laurel's mother got them the job, then," I said, thinking. "Lucky break for them."

"Yeah," said Sabs, sighing. "Sam's team is making out like bandits by selling store-bought cookies, and Stacy's team manages to get paid for a really easy job. What I keep wondering is, when will our team get its lucky break?"

Chapter Seven

"Now, you're sure you're okay here, Allison?" asked my mother for what seemed like the hundredth time that evening.

"Great, Mom," I reassured her again. "Everything will be fine. Don't worry."

It was Friday night. Mary Birdsong was at her psychology study group, and my grandparents had left for their visit to the reservation that afternoon. Some friends of my parents had called a little while before and offered them two tickets to a play at the Acorn Falls Playhouse. Charlie had invited a friend over for the evening, a little black girl named Alexa, so I was going to be home with Charlie, Alexa, and Barrett for the evening. My parents were going to pay me for baby-sitting, so I figured this was a good opportunity to polish up my baby-sitting skills, and to make some money for the Give-a-Thon.

"All right, then, there's plenty of food in the fridge for everyone. Barrett should get a bottle around eight-thirty," Mom said. She pulled on her long navy-blue coat and tucked her purse under her arm.

"Have a good time," said my father, waving, as he opened the front door for her.

"Okay, bye!" I called, carrying Barrett into the den, where Charlie and Alexa were watching TV. I put Barrett in her playpen, and laid one of her stuffed animals beside her. She wriggled around a little and flashed a pretty smile. I smiled back at her. Sometimes she can be so cute.

Just then the phone rang.

"Hello?" I said, picking up the receiver on the desk.

"Hello," said a woman's voice on the other line. "May I please speak with Allison Cloud?"

"This is she," I answered, wondering who it could be.

"Oh, thank goodness," the woman sighed. "Allison, this is Mrs. Ostroy. I live down the street."

"Oh, yes, hello, Mrs. Ostroy," I said. Mrs. Ostroy and my mom were in the PTA together. Mrs. Ostroy had four children: four-year-old twins, named Emily and David, a seven-year-old boy, named Peter, and a ten-year-old girl, whose name was Allison, also.

"I saw your ad for baby-sitting on the bulletin board at Andersen's Bakery," she went on. "Now, I know this is very last-minute, but is there any way I might be able to hire you to baby-sit for a while tonight?"

"Oh," I said, feeling disappointed, "I'm sorry, but I have to stay at home tonight. You see, I'm already taking care of my own brother and sister."

"Oh, but that's perfect!" she said. "You see, my seven-year-old, Peter, is sick with the flu, and the doctor wants me to bring him to the emergency room right away. The trouble is, I don't want to leave the twins home alone with my Allison. My husband is on his way home right now, but he needs to come to the hospital with me. Could I please leave the kids with you? Don't worry, my Allison will be able to help you. She's very good with the twins."

"Um, sure," I said. "Since my parents know you, I guess that would be fine."

After all, I thought, what difference could a couple of more kids make? Besides, it was an chance to make some money for the Give-a-Thon. On the other hand, I had never baby-sat for six kids at once!

"Oh, wonderful," said Mrs. Ostroy, relieved. "You're an absolute lifesaver. As soon as my husband arrives, he'll bring the kids over."

Ten minutes later the doorbell rang.

"Coming!" I called, leaving my book facedown on the couch to mark my place and heading out into the foyer. Charlie, Alexa, and Ralph followed close behind me.

I opened and saw Mr. Ostroy in his black fireman's raincoat and a red fire hat. He held Emily and David by each hand, while Allison stood behind him.

The twins were dressed in different clothing. Emily had on a cute striped outfit, while David wore jeans, a T-shirt, and a baseball jacket.

"Hi, Allison. Well, here we are." Mr. Ostroy said when I opened the door.

Then Mr. Ostroy gently pushed the twins into the foyer and stepped aside so Allison could walk in. "Thanks a lot," he went on, "you're making things a whole lot easier for us. One of us will be by to pick the kids up later. Here is the number where we can be reached at the hospital in case you need us. I'm sorry this is so rushed, but it's an emergency."

Before I could say a word, he had turned around and was gone.

"Well!" I said brightly, looking down at everyone. "Hello, Emily, David, and Allison. Remember me —"

But before I even finished my sentence, I heard crying coming from the den.

"Ohmygosh! Barrett!" I said. I left everyone where they were standing and rushed into the den.

When I got to the den, Barrett was still in her playpen, but she was crying at the top of her lungs. I rushed over and picked her up and she stopped crying immediately. I felt incredibly relieved that she was all right.

"Come on, Barrett," I said, propping her on my hip.

I hurried back to the foyer and found Charlie, Alexa, the twins, and Ralph running around the hallway in circles. The other Allison was trying to catch the twins but wasn't having much success. As soon as Barrett saw all the commotion, she started to cry again.

"Charlie!" I called sternly, bouncing Barrett on my hip to try to get her to stop crying. "Charlie, come here!"

He must have been able to tell how serious I was by the sound of my voice, because he stopped running and came over to me right away, with Ralph close behind him. The other kids quieted down right away.

"Allie, this is fun!" he panted, grinning up at me. "I like these kids!"

"Listen, Charlie," I said, looking down at him sternly, "I really need your help here. Running around and making a lot of noise like this might be fun, but it has to stop now. Look, you guys made Barrett cry."

"Oh, Barrie, don't cry," he said, giving her little tearstained chin a poke with his finger.

Barrett stopped crying, looked at Charlie's grinning face, and let out a smile.

"Okay, listen, Charlie," I said, relieved that Barrett had calmed down, "I'm going to need a lot of help from you tonight. I'm counting on you, okay?"

"Okay, Allie," said Charlie, his chest swelling with pride. "What do you want me to do?"

"I want you to take Emily and David and Alexa into the den to play, okay?" I asked.

"Okay, Allie. What about *that* Allison? What will she do?"

"Don't worry, Charlie," I said, patting his head, "I'll think of something."

Charlie flashed me a smile and called to his new friends, "Come on, guys! Come see our den!" And the two little boys and two little girls ran off into the other room.

"Whew!" I said, and turned to Allison. "I think it's going to be a long night."

She giggled. "You're not kidding. Sometimes the twins get completely out of control."

"Well, if they're anything like my brother, Charlie, I know just what you mean. Hey, listen, why don't you call me Allie, and I'll call you Allison? Is that okay?"

"Sure, Allie, no problem," she said, giving me another smile.

"Well, come on, Allison, let's get into the den before it's destroyed!" I said.

We went into the den, where I put Barrett down in her playpen. The minute I set her down, she started to cry again.

"Barrett, honey, what is it?" I said, picking her up again. Then I looked at my watch. Eight forty-five! My mother had said to give her a bottle at eight-thirty. She must be hungry. Come to think of it, I was kind of hungry, too.

I looked at Charlie, Alexa, and the twins, who were involved with their toys. Allison had settled on the couch and was doing her homework. Things seemed pretty calm. Maybe this was a good time for me to go into the kitchen and get something for everyone to eat.

I lifted Barrett out of her playpen.

"Allison," I said softly, heading toward the door. "I'm going to go get us something to eat. You take care of things while I'm gone, okay?"

She looked up from her notebook and nodded.

I carried Barrett into the kitchen and took her bottle out of the refrigerator. While it was heating up, I grabbed the bread and some peanut butter and jelly. Every kid likes peanut butter and jelly, I figured, and besides, it's probably best to make something really simple so I can get back to the den as soon as possible.

It was kind of hard to make the sandwiches, since Barrett wouldn't let me put her down. I only had one free hand, but I managed. When I finished the sandwiches, I put them onto a tray, along with four glasses of milk and a couple of napkins. Then I took Barrett's bottle out of the water heating on the stove and set it on the tray. I suddenly realized that I couldn't carry everything at once, so I set Barrett down in her infant seat. Of course, she started crying right away. I felt horrible about leaving her crying even for a second, but there wasn't anything I could do. I picked up the tray and quickly carried it to the den, and then I ran back to get Barrett.

I guess I wasn't paying attention the first time I went into the den, but as I went into the room a second time, I heard arguing and commotion. Oh, no, I thought, what's going on now?

It was even worse than I imagined. David and Emily weren't playing; they were fighting over one of the dolls. Allison was kneeling on the couch, trying to calm down Emily, while Alexa was scrambling around, trying to pick up the dolls, stuffed animals, and cars that were scattered all over the floor. Charlie was nowhere to be seen. As soon as Alexa saw me, she ran over to me. She had decided that she wanted to play with the baby and started tugging on my sleeve.

"I tried to stop them, Allie, but I couldn't," Allison said. "David tried to take the doll away from Emily and then they started hitting each other. Then Charlie got upset and ran out of the room."

"It's okay, Allison. It's not your fault. Don't worry about Charlie. I'll find him in a second. Tell you guys what," I said, smiling at them. "Let's all clean up this stuff now and then you can have some peanut butter and jelly sandwiches. I'll go get Charlie and then I'll tell you a story."

I couldn't believe how well it worked. Alexa and Emily helped David and Allison put away the cars and dolls. I found Charlie upstairs in his room, playing calmly with his toys. After a little persuasion, he found his favorite storybook and came back downstairs to join the others.

A little while later Allison, Alexa, and the twins were sitting on the couch, happily munching on their sandwiches. I held Barrett on my lap, feeding her her bottle, and Charlie lay on his stomach on the floor in front of me. He had been so helpful that I didn't say anything when he decided to share his sandwich with Ralph.

I read them a Chippewa folktale about a little girl who learns to speak the language of the animals. She makes friends with all the creatures of the forest, and whenever she goes into the woods, they protect her.

By the time I finished the story, everyone had

finished eating and had fallen asleep. Barrett was sleeping in my arms. Charlie and Alexa had fallen asleep on the floor. Emily and David were curled up on either end of the couch, their mouths slightly open. Even Allison had drifted off to sleep. It was amazing how angelic they all looked. It was hard to imagine that they could have been such little devils when they were awake.

Wow, I thought as I chewed the peanut butter and jelly sandwich, what a tough night! I had no idea it would be this difficult to take care of six kids. In a way it had been fun, too. But I realized that things really could have gone smoothly if I had had some help, though, like if Randy, Katie, and Sabs had been around to give me a hand.

Suddenly I knew the answer to our Give-a-Thon problem! I couldn't wait to call my friends and tell them all about it.

Chapter Eight

"Okay, wait," Randy said, sitting down on the floor of my room and leaning back against my bed, "let me get this straight — you're saying we should put up more signs around town, only this time we're supposed to try to get all the mothers to bring their kids to us?"

"That's right," I said, sitting back in my desk chair and pulling my knees up to my chest. "We pick a day, I was thinking maybe next Saturday, and we advertise a kind of 'activities day' for kids. You know, where we take care of them and do stuff with them. That way, parents can just drop off their children with us and use the day to go shopping or do errands."

It was Saturday, the day after my baby-sitting adventure, and Randy, Sabrina, Katie, and I were in my room. I had just finished telling them about my new idea to raise money for the Give-a-Thon.

"I guess it would be almost like that car-

81

wash thing we saw the ad for at the library," said Katie, who was lying on her stomach across my bed. "You know, a one-day event."

"It's definitely a good idea," Sabrina said. "Especially if we can get a lot of people to sign up. Then we'd be able to make our money for just one day's work."

"The best part is that we all get to work together," I added. "I mean, it was definitely pretty difficult for me to handle six kids by myself last night, but I learned a lot from it, and I earned twenty-two dollars. And I know that if I had had you guys there, it would have been a lot easier."

"Where are we going to do this, though?" asked Randy. "I mean, we need someplace with a lot of room, don't we?"

"I already asked my parents about it," I said, "and they said it's okay for us to do it here. My grandparents are out of town for a while, and my father has to work. My mother said she and Barrett will be on hand if we need them, but mostly they'll stay out of our way. We even have our first customer — Charlie!" I beamed happily.

"We can use the whole upstairs, as long as we close off my parents' room. And we can also use the backyard, if we want."

"Great," said Sabs. "So, what kind of activities do you think we should do with the kids?"

"Well, someone should definitely do something physical," I said, thinking of the way the younger kids had run around the living room the night before. "I think kids probably have a lot of energy to burn off."

"If it's a nice day outside, I could play some active games with them," suggested Katie. "You know, running games and ball games and stuff."

"Good idea," I said, reaching around to my desk and grabbing my notebook. I wrote "Katie — Games" on a fresh sheet of paper.

"And I could do Drama with them," said Sabrina excitedly.

"That's a great idea," I said, writing it down. "We should probably serve them some kind of snacks, like juice and crackers, and I thought I'd have a story hour for them — maybe even have them make their own books or something. Randy, maybe you could do some kind of music activity."

"Definitely," said Randy, nodding. "Me and the kids'll start our own band."

"But, Randy, don't we need musical instruments for that?" asked Katie doubtfully.

"Really," I said, "I don't know where we could get those."

"No problem," said Randy, grinning. "You just let me worry about that."

"All right," I said, shrugging and writing it down in my notebook, "if you say so."

"I guess we'll need new fliers," said Katie. "Can you make some more, Randy?"

"Sure," said Randy. "What should we have them say?"

"Well, we should list all the activities we're going to do with the kids," I said, thinking. "And the date and the place and all that."

"How much do you think we should charge?" asked Katie.

"How about ten dollars," I suggested.

"Sounds good to me," said Randy.

"We need a catchy name for it," said Sabrina. "You know, something that will get people's attention."

"I know," I said suddenly. "How about Play Day?"

"That's perfect," said Katie.

"Play Day — great," said Randy. "I'll try to get the fliers done as soon as possible."

"Oh, no," groaned Sabs. "I guess this means we're going to be visiting every bulletin board in town again."

"Well," I pointed out, "it'll definitely be worth it if it works."

Early the following Saturday morning I opened my eyes and stretched in bed. I looked at my clock — eight o'clock exactly. This gave me plenty of time to get ready, since Play Day was scheduled to begin at ten o'clock. Randy, Katie, and Sabrina had promised to be over by nine o'clock, but I felt like there was a lot of setting up I could start on before they got here.

I took a deep breath. I hoped this Play Day idea was going to work out. What if no one showed up? True, Randy, Katie, Sabs, and I had put signs all over town, but we had done the same thing with our baby-sitting signs, and hardly anyone had called about that. But this was different, I reminded myself. This time we were really offering parents and kids something special, instead of just waiting for them to call us when they needed us.

I picked out some clothes — a long-sleeved purple-and-white-striped T-shirt, baggy pink overalls, and my pink high-top sneakers. By eight-thirty I headed downstairs to the kitchen.

I found Charlie at the kitchen table. My mother was scrambling eggs at the stove, and Mary was feeding Barrett in her high chair.

"Hi, honey," said my mother, turning from the stove to smile at me. "Ready for some breakfast?"

"I think I'll just have some cereal or something, Mom," I answered, taking the milk out of the refrigerator. "I want to make sure I have time to get everything set up."

"All right," she said, turning back to the pan in front of her. "Now, remember, Allison, Mary and I will be here if you need us. We'll be upstairs in my room."

"Okay, Mom, sure," I said, pouring milk on my cereal and sitting down at the table beside Charlie. "Don't worry, though, I'm sure everything will go fine. Besides, it's not like I'm going to be alone or anything — Randy, Sabrina, and Katie will be here, too."

"I'm sure you girls will do just fine," said my mother, smiling at me.

Just then the phone rang.

"I'll get it," I said, standing up and reaching for the wall phone near the table. "Hello?"

"Hello," said a woman's voice on the other end of the line, "I'm calling about the advertisement I saw for Play Day."

"Yes," I said, feeling kind of excited, "how can I help you?"

"Well, I was planning on bringing my little girl, Jennifer, over for the day, but my car's not working. Could you come and pick Jennifer up and walk her back to your house?"

"Pick her up?" I repeated, wondering if I had heard correctly.

"That's right," said the woman. "You see, I've got a hairdresser's appointment at nine forty-five, and I'm not going to be able to bring her over to you. I'm going to have to take the bus to the hairdresser's instead."

Well, we never advertised a pickup service, I thought to myself. This woman's just going to have to figure out some other way to get her child here. But then I had a thought — what if I told her no and she ended up not having her daughter come to Play Day at all? Didn't every ten dollars count, as far as raising the money for Magic Star went? Besides, who knew how many kids were going to come to Play Day? This woman could be one of our few — or maybe even our only customer!

"I can probably have someone come over and walk her back here in a little while," I said, thinking that after Randy, Katie, and Sabs got here, one of us could just go over there. "Where do you live?"

She gave me an address on Cherry Drive, about six blocks away, and I hung up.

"Everything all right, honey?" asked my mother, lifting Barrett out of her high chair and pulling on her little pink sweater.

"Do you need me to do anything before we go upstairs?" asked Mary, clearing the breakfast dishes.

"No, no, everything's fine," I said. "That was just a parent who needed some help with something."

"Okay. See you later, and good luck!" said my mother.

"Have fun," said Mary, following my mother out of the kitchen.

I quickly finished my cereal and opened the door to the cupboard where I had been keeping the cans of juice and boxes of crackers for Play Day. I opened the boxes of crackers, spread them out on some plates, and put the plates on a tray, along with some napkins. I put the tray on the kitchen table and the juice in the refrigerator to cool. Now we would be all set up for snack time.

Next I went upstairs to my room, which I had decided to use for the book-making activity I was going to lead. As I was rolling up my rug, so it wouldn't get ruined if one of the kids spilled something, I heard footsteps clumping up the back stairs to my room.

"Hi, Allie, it's me!" I heard Randy call out. Randy was right on time.

I stood up and walked over to the french doors that lead to my terrace. Randy appeared at the top of the stairs, grinning. Under her black leather jacket she had on a black turtleneck, black cut-off jeans folded up above the knees, and bright red tights with big black polka dots all over them. In her arms were her skateboard and a big cardboard box filled with stuff.

"Randy," I said, letting her in, "don't tell me you actually skateboarded over here with that big box in your arms!"

"Hey, no problem," she said, grinning.

I shook my head. I had tried skateboarding once, and it was amazing to me that Randy managed to balance on her board at all, let alone with a huge box in her arms.

"What is all that?" I asked, peering into the box.

"These are our instruments," said Randy, wiggling her eyebrows mysteriously. She put the box down in a corner and pulled out an empty round oatmeal box. "Now, this may look like an empty box to you," she said, "but it's really a drum." She took out a pair of wooden chopsticks and beat a quick rhythm on the flat top of the round oatmeal box.

"Oh, Randy, that's great!" I said, laughing.

"Wait till you see this one," she said, pulling out the bottom half of an empty shoe box. Stretched around it, across the opening, were several rubber bands. She pulled on one of them, and I heard a twang. "It's a guitar," she said, grinning as she pulled on the different rubber bands.

"Wow, you've been working hard on this stuff," I said, impressed.

"I've got tons more," she said, running her hand through her spiky black hair. "Tambourines made out of pie plates, maracas made out of paper bags filled with dried beans. We're going to have a blast."

"I thought we'd use Mary's room for your

Music Room," I told her, leading her out of my room and next door to Mary's. "That way, Sabs can have Barrett's room, which is a little bigger, for Drama, and Katie can take the kids out in the backyard for Games."

"What about Charlie's room?" asked Randy, picking up her cardboard box and following me.

I rolled my eyes.

"Forget it," I said. "The only activity Charlie's room is ready for is heavy cleaning."

"Yeah, I guess that doesn't sound like too much fun," cracked Randy.

I giggled, thinking about how surprised the kids would be if we told them that one of the fun activities we had planned for them that day was Cleaning.

We walked into Mary's room and Randy put her box down in a corner.

"There," she said, wiping her hands on her jeans.

"Here you are!" I heard Sabrina's voice say suddenly. "We came up the back stairs and looked for you in your room."

I turned around and saw Sabs and Katie standing in the doorway to Mary's room. Sabs was wearing an oversize green-and-white

Bradley High football jersey that I knew must have belonged to one of her brothers, and a pair of black stretch leggings. Katie had on jeans and a navy-blue sailor-top with a white stripe around the collar. The navy-and-white-striped headband in her hair matched her shirt exactly.

"Hi, guys," I said, smiling. "Welcome to the Play Day Music Room."

"That sounds so official," said Sabrina excitedly. "Where's the Drama Room going to be?"

"Right this way," I said, leading them down the hall to Barrett's room. "I thought we could move the bassinet and changing table back against the wall to give you more space."

"This is going to be great," said Sabrina. "I have a book at home called *Exercises for Actors*, and there are some really fun-sounding acting games in it that I think I can do with the kids."

"I've thought of some great ideas for active games, too," said Katie.

"This is so exciting," said Sabrina, bouncing up and down a little. "I can't wait until our first customer gets here."

"Oh!" I said suddenly. "That reminds me. If we want to get our first customer, one of us has to go over to Cherry Drive and pick her up. A moth-

er called here this morning and said she wanted
to send her daughter for Play Day, but she needed someone to pick her up. I was going to say no
at first, but then I figured it was probably worth it
if it guaranteed us a customer."

"I'll go, Allie," Randy volunteered. "I'm pretty
much set up in Mary's room. That way, you can
stay and help Sabs move the furniture in here."

"Thanks, Randy," I said, smiling at her. "I really appreciate it."

"No problem," said Randy. "You definitely
did the right thing. Gee, I wonder if the little girl
would like a ride on a skateboard?"

I looked at her in alarm.

"Just kidding," she said, grinning. "I'll walk,
don't worry."

Randy took off down the stairs and out the
front door, and Sabs and I lifted Barrett's bassinet
and changing table and moved them to one side
of the room.

"This is great," said Sabrina, surveying the
room. "We have plenty of space to move around.
Now all we need is some kids."

Just then the front doorbell rang.

Chapter Nine

"Okay!" Katie shouted half an hour later, putting up one hand to get everyone's attention. "Are you ready? The next number is — number three!"

I looked at the two rows of children facing each other in my backyard. None of them moved.

"Number three?" Katie said again, looking at the kids. "Who's number three?"

"I think I am," said a little boy with dark curly hair named Ben, taking a step forward from the line.

"Okay," said Katie, smiling at him. She looked at the row of children on the opposite side. "And who's number three on that team? Somebody must be number three over there, too."

I counted quickly in my head.

"I think that's you," I said to a little girl named

Donna. "Go on, it's your turn."

It was ten-thirty. Randy wasn't back from picking up the little girl on Cherry Drive yet, and Sabrina and I were trying to help Katie lead the rest of the Play Day kids in a game of Steal the Bacon.

Each child on the two teams had been given a number, so that for every child on one team with a number, there was another child on the other team with the same number. In between the two teams, sitting in the grass, was a rubber ball. The idea was that when Katie called out a number, the person with that number from each team was supposed to run out and try to get the ball, which was called "stealing" the "bacon." If you made it back to your home team with the ball, and without being tagged by the person from the other team, your team got a point. The only problem was that the kids on both teams kept forgetting their numbers.

Just then Randy walked around the side of the house, holding the hand of a little girl with blond pigtails who looked about five years old.

"Hi, guys," said Randy cheerfully, "this is Jennifer."

At the mention of her name, Jennifer hid behind Randy.

"Jennifer's a little 'S-H-Y,'" Randy whispered

to me, spelling out the word.

"Hi, Jennifer," I said softly, squatting down in front of her. "We're playing a fun game here. Do you want to play, too?"

"I want my mommy," said Jennifer, peeking out from behind Randy, her lower lip trembling.

"You're going to get to see your mommy very soon," I reassured her. "But maybe you want to try the game meanwhile. It's really fun, and I could show you how to play."

I put out my hand, and Jennifer took it.

"We really need you on this team over here," I said, leading her to one of the lines of kids. "Now, your number is six. That means that if you hear the number six called, you should rush right out to try and get that red ball in the middle of the grass there. Then if you run back here with it as soon as you can, maybe your team will get a point."

She looked up at me and nodded, a serious expression on her face.

Suddenly I noticed a girl with straight hair sitting a few feet away, pulling at a few blades of grass.

"Hi," I said, walking over to her. "What's your name?"

"Amanda," she said quietly.

"Don't you want to play?" I asked her.

"This is a baby game," she said, pulling harder at the grass. "This whole thing is for babies. I didn't even want to come here today, but my mom made me."

"Maybe you'll have fun," I told her. "You never know unless you try, right?"

"Oh, I know," she said, looking scornfully over at the game. "Look at those little kids. They don't even know how to play. I've been playing that game for my whole life, and I bet I'm older than any of them."

"How old are you?" I asked, sitting down beside her.

"Nine."

"Nine is pretty old, Amanda," I said, nodding. " I can see what you mean."

Suddenly I had an idea.

"Hey, Katie," I called, "you look like you could use a referee over there to help you out."

Katie looked back at me, and I nodded toward Amanda.

"This is Amanda. She knows this game really well," I said. "She could probably help you with the scoring and stuff."

"Sure, Allison," said Katie, smiling. "I could definitely use some help."

"Oh, okay," said Amanda, getting up and walking over to the game.

"The next number is four!" Katie called, and I watched as Emily and David Ostroy, the twins I had taken care of that night, came running out toward the ball. They were so excited by the idea of running around, though, that they completely forgot about the ball and just kept running around in the grass.

"Get the ball! Get the ball!" yelled their older brother, Peter, from the sidelines. Peter, was the boy who had been sick the week before when Mrs. Ostroy had asked me to take care of the twins. Allison, the older sister, had a sleepover with one of her friends and wasn't coming to Play Day, which was too bad, I thought, because she could have kept Amanda company.

"Just call another number, Katie," I suggested. I knew it was probably best just to let the twins burn off some steam by running around.

Slowly the rest of the kids began to get the hang of the game. I held my breath when Katie called Jennifer's number, hoping that she wouldn't get too upset if she got tagged, but she surprised me by outrunning the boy who was trying to tag her and making it back to her team safely.

"Yay, Jennifer, you got a point!" I cheered, and she beamed back at me, her little blond pigtails bouncing.

By the time the game was over, the kids were pink-faced and out of breath. Ben, the little boy with the curly dark hair, approached me with tears in his eyes.

"What is it?" I asked him, bending down to look in his eyes. "What's the matter?"

"My team didn't win," he said, a tear spilling out and rolling down his cheek.

"Oh, don't worry about that," I said, patting him gently on the back. "You did a great job. Besides, now it's time for Music with Randy. I bet you're going to be really good at that."

His face brightened.

"Come on," I said, taking him by the hand. "Let's go upstairs to the Music Room and see what Randy has for us to do."

Upstairs in Mary's room, Randy had all the kids sit in a circle.

"Okay, guys," she began, reaching into the box full of instruments and pulling out the oatmeal carton and the chopsticks, "who wants to play the drum?"

"Me! Me!" cried Emily and David simultaneously.

"I want the drum," said Ben, his eyes filling up again quickly.

"Well, we only have one drum," said Randy. "But we do have lots of other great instruments, too." She reached into the box again. "Here's a guitar — who wants to play the guitar?"

Jennifer raised her hand shyly.

"I want the drum! I want the drum!" cried one of the twins again.

"No, me!" yelled the other one, taking a swipe at the first one's head with his hand.

I looked at Randy, worried. I knew how the twins could get when they were fighting, and I definitely wanted to avoid it if possible. In addition, Ben looked like he was going to burst into tears if he didn't get the drum.

"Okay, I've got it," said Randy suddenly. "Everybody's going to get to play the drum. And the guitar, and the tambourine, and the maracas, and everything else. That's because we're going to play a special game."

She stood up and walked over to the light

switch on the wall.

"See this?" she said, flicking the lights on and off quickly a few times.

The children stared up at the ceiling, fascinated.

"We're all going to march in a circle, playing our instruments," she went on. "And when I turn the lights on and off like that, everybody has to put down their instruments and grab a new one. Got it?"

The kids nodded and I grinned, impressed with Randy's idea.

It worked out really well. The kids loved marching with their instruments, and they each got to try all of them out. By the time the game was over, everyone was smiling, including the twins and Ben.

Next it was time for Drama with Sabrina, so the four of us lined the kids up and marched them down the hall to Barrett's room.

On our way, Jennifer tugged at my overalls.

"Yes, Jennifer, what is it?" I asked, smiling down at her.

"Is it time for my mommy to come get me yet?" she asked, her forehead wrinkled.

"Not yet," I said, giving her hand a reassuring squeeze. "But pretty soon."

We all filed into Barrett's room and sat down on the rug.

"Hi, everybody," said Sabs, smiling this huge smile. "I'm Sabrina, and I'm going to teach you some new games. These aren't the kinds of games with winners and losers, but they're lots of fun."

I glanced at Ben, who seemed relieved.

"The first game is called the Mirror Game," Sabrina went on, "and in order to play it, you need to find a partner."

Randy, Katie, and I helped the kids divide up into pairs, and Sabrina explained that the idea of the game was for one partner to do everything that the other partner did, like a mirror. The kids could take turns being the leader and being the mirror.

As we got started, there were lots of giggles, and everybody seemed to enjoy it. Everybody except the older girl, Amanda, that is, who was sitting on the sidelines again.

"No way," she said when I went over to try to coax her into the game. "This is for total babies."

I couldn't believe it, but right then and there I got another idea. "Hey, Amanda, follow me."

"Okay," she said with a sigh and followed me out of the room.

We walked down the hall and into my room.

"This is my room, Amanda. Why don't you look through some of my books or magazines and make yourself comfortable."

"Really?" she asked.

"Sure. No problem. You can even go and sit in the swing on the porch, if you want. Make yourself at home."

"Cool! Thanks, Allison." She seemed almost happy now.

"Very good," said Sabrina as I walked back into the Drama Room. "Now it's time to do some pretending. Who here is good at pretending?"

Everyone's hand shot up.

"All right," said Sabrina, pointing to the twins' older brother, Peter. "Why don't you go first? Come on up here, and I'll whisper something for you to pretend. But while you're pretending, you can't say any words, okay? Just use your body. Then we'll see if the rest of the kids can guess what it is you're doing."

She bent over and whispered into Peter's ear.

Peter smiled and sat down cross-legged on

the floor. Looking at the audience of kids, he picked up an imaginary object in his hands.

"You're holding a pencil!" someone called out.

"You're going to draw a picture!" guessed someone else.

Peter shook his head no. Dipping his hand down a little first, he raised the imaginary object to his lips.

"You're eating!" called Ben.

"You're licking a lollipop," said Jennifer.

Suddenly Peter jumped up, dropping his imaginary object. Letting his tongue hang out of his mouth, he fanned it with his hand.

"You just tasted some soup that was too hot!" cried Ben.

"That's it!" said Sabrina, smiling. "Good job, Peter. You too, Ben."

Sabrina led the kids through a few more rounds. The twins got to pretend they were lions in the jungle, which they loved, and Jennifer pretended to be a leaf blowing in the wind.

Suddenly Ben raised his hand.

"Okay, let me give this a try," he said, standing up and walking over to Sabrina.

Sabs whispered in his ear, and he grinned.

Walking to the center of the room, he lay down on the rug on his stomach. For a moment he was perfectly still, and I was beginning to wonder if he was going to do anything at all. Then, slowly, he began to twitch a little bit. His movements got bigger and bigger until he was bouncing around wildly on the floor, flipping from his stomach to his back and back to his stomach again. The kids began to giggle, and by the time he finished, they were shrieking with laughter.

He stood up, grinning, and bowed to his audience.

"Well?" he said, looking at us. "Does anyone know what it was?"

No one said anything. I, for one, had no idea what he had been trying to do.

"I was a piece of bacon frying in a pan!" he announced triumphantly, sending the kids into another fit of giggles.

"Bravo!" called Sabrina, clapping her hands. "That was a really hard one I gave you, Ben, and you were great!"

I had to agree. Ben had definitely given a really good performance. I shook my head, amazed. Who would have guessed that a piece of bacon frying in a pan could be so funny?

Finally it was time for my book-making project. Seeing the kids enjoy themselves all morning had given me a really good idea for it.

With Randy, Katie, and Sabrina's help, I led them all back down the hall to my room, where I passed out the paper and crayons. Out of the corner of my eye, I saw that the older girl, Amanda, had come into the room.

"Well," I began, looking at the group of happy faces around me, "it looks like we've all had a fun day, and I think maybe we should have a special way to remember this day. So, now, each of you is going to get to make your own book all about today."

"Make books?" Peter asked skeptically. "How can we do that?"

"I'm going to show you," I said. "Books are really just pieces of paper attached together, you know. It's the words and pictures inside that make them special."

I took a few sheets of construction paper and stapled them together down one side.

"There," I said, opening the blank "book" to show the children. "Now all it needs is something inside."

"I want to make a book," said Jennifer, her

eyes shining. "But I don't know how to write."

"That's okay," I said. "Those of you who can't write can draw pictures about your day. If you decide you want there to be some words inside about your day, too, Randy, Katie, Sabrina, or I can write them for you. I bet Amanda would be willing to help out, too."

I looked at Amanda, who grinned back at me and nodded.

Randy, Katie, Sabrina, Amanda, and I helped the kids get their books set up, stacking pieces of construction paper and stapling them along the books' "bindings." A hush fell over the room as everyone got to work filling in their books with words and pictures.

After the five of us helped the kids finish their books, Randy and I went downstairs to the kitchen to get their snack. Randy stuck several cans of juice under her arms, and I carried the tray of crackers and glasses back up to my room.

Katie and Sabrina and Amanda helped us pass out the juice and crackers, and the children sat contentedly, munching on their snacks.

Suddenly Jennifer walked up to me, a cracker in her hand.

"When do you think my mommy's going to

come?" she asked. Jennifer climbed into my lap, and looked up at me with her big brown eyes.

I looked at my watch. Play Day had only ten minutes left to go.

"Very, very soon," I told her smiling. "Any minute."

Jennifer's face fell.

"But I don't want to go home yet," she said. "I want to stay here with you."

"I had fun with you today, too, Jennifer," I said.

I looked around my room. Katie was sitting in a corner with Amanda, talking about sports, and Sabs was nearby, playing with Emily and David. Randy was refilling Ben's juice glass.

Wow, I thought, we did it. It wasn't exactly an easy day, but I'd definitely say it was a success.

Chapter Ten

"Hey, Allie, nice outfit," said Randy, grinning.

I looked down at my cropped red-and-white-striped T-shirt, gathered black miniskirt, and black stretch bicycle shorts.

"Why, thank you," I said, grinning back at her. "I got it at Dare."

"That's funny," said Sabrina, her hazel eyes twinkling. "That's where I got my outfit, too!"

She pointed to her ruffled purple top, denim miniskirt, and purple-and-pink-striped tights.

"What a coincidence!" said Katie, giggling and looking down at her own pink polka-dot T-shirt and soft, gray knit leggings. "That's where I got my outfit, too!"

"Me too!" said Randy, turning around to model her daisy-covered black capri pants and black boat-necked T-shirt.

"Come on, you guys," I said, laughing, "let's go inside."

It was Friday evening, six days after Play Day, and the Give-a-Thon Contest was over. Randy, Katie, Sabs, and I were standing outside Rob's Rollers.

"You know," said Katie as the four of us walked toward the front door, "I think winning second prize in the contest really worked out well for us after all."

"Me too," agreed Randy. "I mean, we got to get all these great new clothes at Dare, and we still get to go to the rollerblading party, too."

"That's true," said Sabrina. "But somehow I still wish it could have happened without Sam's team winning like that. He's been walking around the house with this really smug expression ever since the results were announced in school yesterday — just because his team managed to make two hundred and seventy-nine dollars for the Give-a-Thon."

"The boys just had a lot of lucky breaks," I said. "But we came up with a really good idea, and I think we did really well, too."

"That's for sure," said Randy. "After all, we raised two hundred and ten dollars."

"Definitely," said Katie. "And it was for a really good cause, too."

"Hey," said Randy, pulling open the door, "did you guys see Stacy's face when she realized her team had come in third and won the tickets to that nature lecture series at the museum?"

"She definitely didn't look too happy," Sabs said, giggling and followed Randy inside.

"I bet Laurel's mother makes them all go, too," said Katie. "I'm pretty sure the Ladies' Garden Club is one of the museum's biggest members."

We walked into the roller rink and looked around. There were tons of kids everywhere, and loud music was playing. The rink itself was lit up by lots of blinking colored lights, and there was a giant ball covered with tiny mirrors hanging in the middle of the ceiling. As the mirrored ball spun around, little speckles of light flew everywhere.

"Wow," said Sabrina, looking around. "This is really amazing!"

"Really," agreed Randy, "pretty cool."

"Come on," I said, spotting a desk a little way away with a neon sign that said SKATE GEAR above it, "let's go get our roller blades."

We took off our shoes and turned them in at the desk for four pairs of roller blades, knee pads, and elbow pads.

"Wow," said Katie, pulling the laces on her roller blades, "these really are a lot like ice skates."

I pulled on my purple-and-white knee pads and elbow pads and slipped my feet into the shiny black skates with the purple wheels, wondering how I was ever going to manage to stand up on these things.

"Hey," said Randy, looking down at my hands as I laced my skates, "that's a really cool-looking ring, Allie. Is it new?"

I looked down at the silver ring shaped like a butterfly on my finger.

"Mary Birdsong gave it to me," I explained. "It's a thank-you present for helping her study for her psychology exam — she got an A."

Just then Sam came flying toward us, totally out of control on his skates.

"Hey, watch out," said Sabrina as her twin crashed into the bench, practically knocking her over.

"Hi, Sabs," said Sam, grinning. "Wow, these things are great — almost as much fun as skateboarding, Randy — wait till you guys try them."

He pulled himself off the bench and skated away, still wildly out of control, but somehow managing not to fall.

"This is great!" said Katie, standing up easily and gracefully skating a few yards away.

"Okay, here goes," said Sabrina, pulling herself up quickly by holding on to the bench. Almost right away her feet slipped out from under her, and she fell on her backside on the floor.

"Ouch!" she said, grinning up at us."That smarts."

I pulled myself carefully into a standing position and held on to the railing that surrounded the skating area.

"Way to go, Allie!" said Randy, grinning at me as I managed to let go and stand on my own.

"Keep your weight forward if possible," Katie instructed. "That way, if you fall down, you'll fall forward and be able to break the fall with your hands."

"Now she tells us," said Sabrina, rolling her eyes.

Carefully I let go of the railing and moved a few feet on my own. I was definitely starting to get the hang of this. Suddenly I felt someone come up behind me and put his hands on my waist.

"How're you doing, Allison?" a voice asked.

I turned my head and saw Billy behind me. He was wearing a blue baseball cap backward on his head, and he was smiling, his blue eyes shining.

"Oh, hi, Billy," I said, smiling back at him. "It's not exactly easy, but I think I'm getting a little better at it."

"Hey, this is fun," said Billy as we whipped around a corner together.

I smiled and nodded in agreement.

"Wow, look at Katie and Scottie," I said, nodding my head toward the other side of the rink.

Katie and Scottie were skating about twice as fast as anyone else, and what made it even more incredible was that they were skating backward! Katie was grinning, and I could tell she was really having a good time.

"Amazing," said Billy, shaking his head.

Sam suddenly skated past us, grabbed Billy's baseball cap off his head, and took off with it.

"Hey!" Billy called after him. He turned to me. "Excuse me, Allison, but this means war."

I laughed, watching Billy skate as fast as he could, chasing Sam through the crowd of people.

At that moment Randy skated up beside me.

"Hey, Allie, you're doing really well on those things," she said, nodding down at my roller blades.

"It's fun," I said, shrugging.

She looked over at Sabrina, who was still struggling, holding on to the railing on the other side of the rink.

"Come on," she said, grabbing my hand. "Let's go get Sabs and show her a good time."

We skated around the rink and up behind Sabrina, each grabbing on to one of her hands.

"Aaah! You guys scared me," she said, almost falling over.

"Okay, Sabs, it's time for you to build up a little speed," said Randy, pulling Sabrina by the hand.

"Oh, no," said Sabrina, laughing and shrieking. "What are you trying to do to me?!"

"Don't worry, Sabs, we won't let you fall," I said, pulling on her other hand.

Randy and I skated faster, pulling the laughing Sabrina between us. Suddenly I felt Katie skate up beside me.

"Hey, can I join the chain, too?" she asked.

"Sure, Katie, come on," I said, holding out my other hand.

Together, the four of us skated faster and faster around the rink, whipping around the corners. As the music played and the colored lights bounced off my friends' smiling faces, I thought about how much fun the contest had been and how proud I was of how well we had done. But mostly I thought about how lucky I was to have the three best friends in the whole world.

Don't Miss
GIRL TALK #43
KATIE'S BEVERLY HILLS FRIEND

I was really looking forward to Erica's visit. She had written me almost every day when she first moved, although now she wrote only about once a month. Her letters told me all about what it was like to live in Beverly Hills, and my letters kept her up-to-date on all the news from Acorn Falls. There had been a lot of news for me to write, too. First I had quit the flag squad and joined the hockey team — the *boys'* hockey team. Then my mother got remarried — to a French-Canadian man named Jean-Paul Beauvais, whose son, Michel, is also in the seventh grade. Michel and I were on the hockey team together, so we got to be good friends as well as stepbrother and stepsister. Then my mother, Emily, and I moved from the little house where we'd always lived to a much larger house. Jean-Paul owns a big advertising agency and is very successful. All of this added up to a lot of changes, and it sure took some getting used to. I often wrote to Erica to help sort out my feelings about everything.

Whenever I saw a lavender envelope in our mailbox, I got excited because I knew it was Erica's stationery. But there was one side of Erica's visit that I wasn't looking forward to, and this encounter in the hallway had just brought it out into the open. That letter Stacy was reading out loud to her friends just now was written on lavender stationery. Obviously Erica had also written to Stacy, telling her that she was coming for a visit.

But I couldn't help wondering — how would I handle Erica, Stacy and her group, and my new friends, too?

TALK BACK!
TELL US WHAT YOU THINK ABOUT
GIRL TALK BOOKS

Name _____

Address _____

City _____ State _____ Zip_____

Birthday _____ Mo._____ Year _____

Telephone Number (____)_____

1) Did you like this GIRL TALK book?

Check one: YES_____ NO_____

2) Would you buy another GIRL TALK book?

Check one: YES_____ NO_____

If you like GIRL TALK books, please answer questions 3-5;
otherwise go directly to question 6.

3) What do you like most about GIRL TALK books?

Check one: Characters_____ Situations_____
          Telephone Talk_____Other_____

4) Who is your favorite GIRL TALK character?

Check one: Sabrina_____ Katie_____ Randy_____
Allison_____ Stacy_____ Other (give name) _____

5) Who is your *least* favorite character?

_____

6) Where did you buy this GIRL TALK book?

Check one: Bookstore____Toy store____Discount store____
Grocery store___Supermarket___Other (give name)_____

Please turn over to continue survey.

7) How many GIRL TALK books have you read?
Check one: 0____   1 to 2____   3 to 4 ____   5 or more____

8) In what type of store would you look for GIRL TALK books?
Bookstore_____Toy store_____Discount store_____
Grocery store_____Supermarket_____Other (give name)_____

9) Which type of store would you visit most often if you wanted to buy a GIRL TALK book?
Check *only* one: Bookstore_____Toy store_____
Discount store_____Grocery store_____Supermarket_____
Other (give name)_____

10) How many books do you read in a month?
Check one: 0____   1 to 2____   3 to 4 ____   5 or more____

11) Do you read any of these books?
Check those you have read:
The Baby-sitters Club_____   Nancy Drew_____
Pen Pals_____ Sweet Valley High _____
Sweet Valley Twins_____Gymnasts_____

12) Where do you shop most often to buy these books?
Check one: Bookstore_____Toy store_____
Discount store_____Grocery store_____Supermarket_____
Other (give name)_____

13) What other kinds of books do you read most often?
_____

14) What would you like to read more about in GIRL TALK?
_____
_____

Send completed form to :
GIRL TALK Survey, Western Publishing Company, Inc.
1220 Mound Avenue, Mail Station #85
Racine, Wisconsin 53404

**LOOK FOR THE AWESOME GIRL TALK BOOKS IN
A STORE NEAR YOU!**

MORE GIRL TALK TITLES TO LOOK FOR

Nonfiction
ASK ALLIE 101 answers to your questions about boys, friends, family, and school!

YOUR PERSONALITY QUIZ Fun, easy quizzes to help you discover the real you!

BOYTALK: HOW TO TALK TO YOUR FAVORITE GUY